LITTLE WHITE LIES

Other books in the
CANTERWOOD CREST SERIES:

TAKE THE REINS

CHASING BLUE

BEHIND THE BIT

TRIPLE FAULT

BEST ENEMIES

CANTERWOOD CREST

LITTLE WHITE LIES

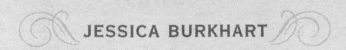

JESSICA BURKHART

ALADDIN M!X

New York London Toronto Sydney

This book is a work of fiction. Any references to historical events, real people, or real locales are used fictitiously. Other names, characters, places, and incidents are the product of the author's imagination, and any resemblance to actual events or locales or persons, living or dead, is entirely coincidental.

ALADDIN M!X
Simon & Schuster Children's Publishing Division
1230 Avenue of the Americas, New York, NY 10020
First Aladdin M!X edition December 2009
Text copyright © 2009 by Jessica Burkhart
All rights reserved, including the right of reproduction
in whole or in part in any form.
ALADDIN is a trademark of Simon & Schuster, Inc., and related logo
is a registered trademark of Simon & Schuster, Inc.
ALADDIN M!X and related logo are registered trademarks
of Simon & Schuster, Inc.
For information about special discounts for bulk purchases, please
contact Simon & Schuster Special Sales at 1-866-506-1949
or business@simonandschuster.com.
The Simon & Schuster Speakers Bureau can bring authors to your live event.
For more information or to book an event contact the Simon & Schuster Speakers
Bureau at 1-866-248-3049 or visit our website at www.simonspeakers.com.
Designed by Jessica Handelman
The text of this book was set in Venetian 301 BT.
Manufactured in the United States of America
14 16 18 19 20 17 15
Library of Congress Control Number 2009937541
ISBN 978-1-4169-9038-3
ISBN 978-1-4169-9831-0 (eBook)
0423 OFF

To the photo shoot crew—
Jessica Handelman, Karin Paprocki,
Russell Gordon, Monica Stevenson, and her assistants;
Kate Angelella; and the Canterwood models.
Thank you for creating this gorgeous cover!

ACKNOWLEDGMENTS

Kate Angelella, you're a supertalented editor who makes every book better than I even imagined it could be. And I'm not saying that just because we did this book's edit letter over manis and pedis. Nope. ☺

Alyssa Henkin, thank you for working hard on all things Canterwood.

Thanks doesn't begin to cover it to the amazing team at Simon & Schuster. Thank you, Mara Anastas, Fiona Simpson, and Bethany Buck for backing Canterwood. Thanks to Bess Braswell, Lucille Rettino, and Venessa Williams for their marketing genius. Nicole Russo, I still feel superimportant when I tell people you're my publicist. Thank you to Brenna Franzitta, production editor extraordinaire. Thanks to Jessica Handelman, Russell Gordon, Monica Stevenson, and the models.

Thanks to my friends who have welcomed me to the city, especially Aly Heller and Liesa Abrams. Mandy Morgan, come visit already! Lauren Barnholdt, "Team Barnhart," FTW!

Ross, you're the coolest guy I know and just thinking about our neighborhood adventures makes me smile.

Kate, a better BFF doesn't exist. Life would be *so* sparkle-free without you. LYSMB!

Finally, to the reader girlies who chat on the forums, e-mail me, send pics, and create videos—I heart you all! Team Canterwood!

LITTLE WHITE LIES

YOU CALL THIS A WELCOME?

I'D BEEN BACK ON THE CANTERWOOD CREST Academy campus for an hour and I already felt trapped. Not a feeling I'd imagined experiencing on my first day of eighth grade.

But it was true. If I left my dorm, I could get caught between Jacob—my ex–almost-boyfriend who suddenly wanted me back—and Eric—my amazing boyfriend who still didn't know that Jacob had confessed his feelings to me the day before summer break.

I sat at the edge of my still-unmade bed and took a deep breath, wanting to stay in the safety of my room. I wished my BFF and roommate, Paige Parker, would hurry through her parental good-byes. I needed girl advice stat!

I considered the possibilities:

Out There—I might run into Jacob. That was not good. But I *also* wanted to see Eric, and with the "no boys allowed in Winchester Hall—ever!" rule, running into him here was highly unlikely. Unless he wanted to risk death by Livvie, my dorm monitor.

Plus, even though I didn't want to leave, I kind of had to. My riding coach, Mr. Conner, was holding a team meeting at the stable in half an hour. I couldn't risk being late—it was the first meeting for the Youth Equestrian National Team. After spending most of my summer riding at YENT camp, there was no way I could be late to the first meeting.

I stepped around my matching pink suitcases and checked my reflection in the full-length mirror, wanting to look pretty but casual when I saw Eric for the first time since before summer vacay. I ran my fingers through my light brown hair and flicked a stray eyelash off my cheek. A coat of Cherry Blossom gloss was all I needed—it was so hot outside that any more makeup would run.

I peeled off the wrinkled shirt I'd worn on the two-hour drive from home and pulled a new one from my open suitcase. The cotton-candy pink "I ♥ New York" baby tee looked cute with my jean skirt. I'd gotten the T-shirt when I spent a couple of weeks this summer in NYC with Paige.

I smiled as I looked around our room—glad that we'd gotten approval to be roommates again in our familiar seventh-grade dorm room. Despite my worry about running into Jacob, I was beginning to feel better about being here.

Going 2 the stbl 4 mtg. U? I texted Eric.

I pulled on my paddock boots and glanced at my laptop. *Just one quick check for any school announcements,* I told myself.

Zero new messages.

The mouse hovered over my "save these!!" folder. After a moment's hesitation, I clicked on the message I'd been staring at all summer long. *From: Jacob Schwartz. Subject: Sasha, please read. 6/27. 7:46 p.m.*

There was no reason to open that e-mail. None. I should have deleted it the second I'd gotten it this summer. After all, I had a boyfriend. Only horrible girlfriends saved e-mails from other guys—especially other guys currently dating their BFFs. What was wrong with me? But instead of erasing the message, I opened it and read it for the thousandth time.

Sasha,
I had to try again to tell you how sorry I am
for the way I acted at the Sweetheart Soirée.

I know you're with Eric and I'm dating Callie,
but I can't give up. Not when I still like you so
much. You know I don't want to hurt Callie
and I'm sure you feel the same about Eric, but
you can't ignore the truth—there's something
between us. I hope you e-mail or text me back
or something. If not, I'll see you at school. Have
a great time at YENT camp.

—Jacob

Not that I'd needed to read the e-mail again to know what it said. I'd had it for three months and now every single word had become stuck in my brain. Just like the look on his face when he'd found me in the courtyard minutes before I'd left to go home last year—the first time he'd told me he wanted me back. I'd run from him then, not answering, and hadn't replied to any of his messages all summer.

My phone buzzed and I jumped. With shaky fingers, I grabbed my phone.

BRT! Can't wait 2 c u.

Eric. He was the guy I wanted, not Jacob. Just thinking about seeing Eric after a summer apart made me grin. I couldn't wait to see his creamy coffee-brown skin and his thick, dark hair that sometimes fell in front of his eyes.

Jacob would have to figure out how to deal.

I shut down the computer and left the dorm, hurrying down the glossy wooden floors of the hallway and stepping around luggage that was stacked outside dorm room doors. Eric was waiting for me. What happened with Jacob—his confession, the e-mail—none of it mattered. Eric and I were happy together. Jacob was too late.

2

EVERY GIRL
FOR HERSELF

I LEFT WINCHESTER AND WALKED DOWN THE sidewalk, enjoying the sun and warm late-August air. The campus was much calmer this weekend than it had been this time last year. The newbies had moved in yesterday and returning students were arriving over the weekend. As I looked around, I realized just how much I'd missed Canterwood over the summer. I tried to take in every bit of campus as I walked.

Full oak and maple trees shaded the freshly painted wooden benches that dotted the pristine lawn. Black, old-fashioned streetlamps lined the sidewalks that snaked around the state-of-the-art dorms, gym, media center, pool, tennis courts, and stable. A stone wall covered in ivy encircled most of campus.

I hurried down the sloping hill and walked into the stable, scanning the main aisle for Eric. Bay, chestnut, gray, and roan horses filled every available pair of cross-ties and glossy tack trunks with brass locks were lined up in front of the stalls. I walked through the center of the stable, passed the hot walker, and grinned.

Eric stood in the aisle, looking beyond adorable in a red T-shirt with a frayed hem and cargo shorts. His light brown skin had darkened over the summer and I thought he maybe even looked taller.

"Eric!" I called.

He turned his head. "Hey!"

I didn't care if Mr. Conner caught me running in the stable and made me muck out stalls till I was twenty—I darted forward and threw myself into Eric's arms. We hugged each other and I squeezed him hard, not wanting to let go. We pulled back. I couldn't stop looking at him. Everything about him was familiar—the way he smelled like spearmint and dryer sheets, his easy, laid-back smile, and the way I fit into his body when we hugged.

"Missed you," he said, his dark brown eyes locked on mine.

"Me too."

Eric leaned in to kiss me and, for a second, I hesitated.

You're just nervous, I told myself. *You haven't kissed him in months!* It's not like someone can forget how to kiss over the summer. I closed my eyes and brushed my lips against his. We smiled at each other.

"I'm glad to see you," Eric said. "But was starting school a week early part of the evil plan to eventually make school last *all* year?"

I laughed. "Knowing the headmistress, probably. But at least fall break isn't too far off this year."

Eric squeezed my hand. "True. And that's only a week long. Not like spending all summer apart. Seven days is much better."

"Agreed." I blushed and looked into the stall in front of us. Inside was Luna, the school horse Eric usually rode.

"She looks great," I said. The flea-bitten gray mare bumped Eric's elbow playfully with her muzzle. She had a total crush on him.

Eric rubbed her forehead. "I really missed her this summer. I'm going to groom her, and then go meet Troy for pizza at The Slice."

"And I better get to my meeting. Text you later?"

I tossed a final smile over my shoulder at Eric. He grinned back and I felt his eyes on me as I walked away. The nerves about being around him would go away—I knew I just needed time after being separated all summer.

I left Eric and walked to the skybox. When I got there, Heather Fox and Jasmine King were already waiting. Both girls sat at opposite ends of the room with their arms folded. The leader of the Trio and the transfer from Wellington Preparatory had a long history of hating each other. For years, they'd competed against each other with both girls battling for first place in every big show on the toughest circuit. Now that Jasmine was at Canterwood, Heather had stepped up her game—something I hadn't even known was possible.

Heather's blond hair was in a messy French braid and her skin bronzed from a summer in the sun. She looked over at me and half-smiled. For Heather, that counted as superfriendly.

Jasmine's dark hair tumbled in loose waves around her shoulders and she focused her eyes on me. Unlike Heather's, Jas's skin was pale and peachy blush high-lighted her cheekbones.

"Your letter get lost in the mail?" Jas asked, smoothing her ruffled black skirt.

I sat next to Heather and looked six seats down to Jasmine. "What letter?"

She rolled her eyes toward the ceiling. "The one from the YENT where they told you that your offer to join the team was revoked after—oh, yeah—they came to their senses and realized what a loser rider you are."

I sat back in my chair and blew out a breath. As if I'd expected this year with Jas to go any other way, especially after how she'd acted during YENT camp over the summer. She couldn't deal with having me—a "loser" rider—at the ultra-exclusive camp for one of the most prestigious riding teams in the country. Jas hadn't stopped going after me for one second during all six weeks of camp. And I'd been alone.

But that, I reminded myself, was my fault. Callie Harper, my other BFF and former riding teammate, wasn't on the YENT because of me. Jacob had been acting weird for weeks before YENT testing last spring and Callie had obsessed about what was going on with him. Neither of us knew that it had been because Jacob wanted me back. Callie's riding had been off on test day and it had cost her a spot on the YENT. Callie still didn't know the truth—and as long as I had it my way, she never would.

Mr. Conner strode into the room. "Welcome back, girls," he said. His dark hair had been cropped shorter over the summer and he wore a hunter green polo shirt with *CCA* stitched in gold thread over his heart.

"Hi," we all said.

He eyed our seating choices, but didn't comment. "I'm glad to see all of you back at school. I hope you're ready to get started on Monday."

Heather and I glanced at each other. He'd been tough on us when we'd been riders on his advanced team—when Callie had been on our team—and there was no question that he'd be even tougher on us now.

"Since you're all riding for the Youth Equestrian National Team," Mr. Conner continued, "your schedule will be different from last year's." He picked up a leather-bound binder, opened it, and consulted a page. "You will not have morning lessons."

"Yes!" Heather, Jasmine, and I all whispered at the same time.

Mr. Conner tilted his head, looking at us.

Oops.

But he grinned and we all started laughing. No morning lessons meant I could actually sleep in a little and not rush to shower, change, and get dressed before class every morning.

"Don't get too excited. Your afternoon class will be

longer and more intense," Mr. Conner said. "To accommodate this schedule, I've hired an assistant coach to teach the beginning riders. Ms. Walker starts on Monday. Please welcome her when you see her around. Also, I will have to submit written progress reports directly to Mr. Nicholson every other week."

So if I had a bad practice, would that go in my progress report? *Gulp.* Charm and I had to be *on* every day. I never wanted Mr. Nicholson to think he'd made a mistake in choosing me for the advanced team. Especially after my riding hadn't been up to my usual standards at YENT camp.

Mr. Conner flipped to a different page in his binder. "As the head scout of the YENT, Mr. Nicholson expects written reports as well as visual proof that you are all progressing in the program."

"Will he come from Lexington to watch us ride?" Heather asked.

"No," Mr. Conner said. "Each month, I'll record a lesson and e-mail him the file. He'll watch it and make notes about each of you. Since this is the first time Canterwood has had the honor of students riding for the YENT, we will all make sure to represent Canterwood Crest Academy's riding team to the best of our abilities."

Talk about pressure . . .

Jasmine raised her hand and her silver bangles clattered down her arm. "Mr. Conner?"

He nodded at her. "Yes?"

"When's our first show?" Jas asked.

"The first few weeks will be about settling into the new schedule and practicing," Mr. Conner said. "We will not begin the fall show schedule until later in the semester— not until every rider is prepared and at her best."

A look crossed Jasmine's face as if she wanted to argue, but instead she slumped into her seat, not saying another word. But I was relieved. I needed any extra practice I could get—Charm and I were going to prove ourselves to Mr. Conner and Mr. Nicholson.

"When we do kick off the showing season," Mr. Conner said, "we'll start with a schooling show as a warm-up for future events."

Jasmine huffed. "A *schooling* show?"

Mr. Conner's eyes narrowed on Jasmine and her fair cheeks turned the color of my shirt. "Jasmine, the level of competition for the YENT surpasses that of the advanced team by leaps and bounds. We will *not* be showing before Mr. Nicholson and I decide the team is ready."

So, ha! I wanted to add.

"Rest up over the weekend—you're going to need to be ready to work on Monday afternoon," Mr. Conner said. "I suggest you start mapping out your schedules as soon as you can to allow enough time for classes, homework, stable chores, and riding lessons. Come to me if you have questions, all right?"

Each of us nodded as he gathered his papers and binder and left the skybox. Heather and I stood and, together, started for the door.

"No morning lessons is only the best news ever," Heather said.

"Totally," I said. "We can actually get up at a normal hour."

Jasmine followed us out. "Please. This is ridic. *One* lesson a day and a *schooling* show? We're on the YENT now—not the beginner team. A schooling show will be embarrassing."

Heather turned on the stairway. Even though she was two steps lower than Jasmine, she somehow seemed taller. "You talk a big game. Let's see if you're so uberconfident on Monday after we ride."

Jasmine glared at us, and Heather and I headed down the rest of the steps, into the aisle, and away from Jas.

"Later, Silver," Heather said. She was gone before I

could reply, probably off to find Julia and Alison—her BFFs and the other two-thirds of the Trio. But unlike Heather and me, Julia and Alison weren't allowed to ride. They'd been banned from riding since they'd been caught last spring cheating on a history exam. Both girls had denied the cheating and had theories that Jasmine was somehow involved. But without proof, they were grounded, literally, until next January.

I walked to Charm's stall and peered inside. "Hi, boy!" I said.

Charm turned his chestnut head toward me, still munching on stalks of hay. I let myself into the stall and stood on my tiptoes to wrap my arms around his neck. Charm, a Thoroughbred and Belgian mix, was my soon-to-be-nine-year-old gelding. We'd been inseparable since my parents had bought him for me almost four years ago. I ran my finger down his blaze and kissed his cheek.

"Two days is way too long to be apart, huh?" I asked him.

Charm bobbed his head and I leaned into him, glad to have a couple of minutes to think before leaving the stable. I hadn't seen Callie yet, but she'd texted me this morning to say she couldn't wait to see me. I'd missed her a lot over the summer, but more than she knew at YENT camp.

Except for the awful time when Callie and I had been fighting, we'd always been there for each other during shows and lessons. I'd always had one person in the ring who was on my side. But now it was every girl for herself. Heather was still the leader of the Trio and she'd only step up for me if she thought Jas's threats against me were bringing down the team.

Charm stretched his neck to the hay net in the corner. I patted his shoulder and left the stall. I couldn't spend every second worrying about how my riding looked compared to Heather's and Jasmine's. But a nagging voice inside my head reminded me that I hadn't ridden my best at YENT camp and it had showed. Big-time.

My phone vibrated and I flipped it open to see a text from Paige. *In room. Can u stop @ SS 2 pick us up treats?*

Totally! C u in a sec. I sent the message and started for the Sweet Shoppe—Canterwood's amazing café/bakery. I stepped under the old-fashioned blue-and-white-striped awning and into the shop. The smell of brownies, cookies, and cakes was overwhelming. I gave myself thirty seconds to make a decision, otherwise I'd order everything in the shop. The barista smiled at me and I stepped up to the counter.

"Two ice-cream sundaes with extra sprinkles to go, please," I said.

She got two plastic containers and started scooping ice cream into them. I was almost safe and back in my dorm without running into—

"Sasha?"

I turned to find Jacob just feet behind me, his green eyes searching mine. Like Eric, he'd gotten taller over the summer and the sun had streaked his shaggy light brown hair with pieces of honey blond.

"Jacob, I . . . ," I said. "I was just getting my order and leaving."

I looked back at the barista, willing her to serve up the fastest order ever. Jacob stepped closer behind me.

"Can't we just talk for a sec? I didn't hear from you all summer and—"

But I couldn't. Not now. Not last June when he'd told me he still had feelings for me. Not all summer when he'd e-mailed me. I had to get out of here.

Turning away from the counter, I left the barista scooping my sundaes and skirted around Jacob. I shoved open the door and ran for Winchester, dodging people on the sidewalk and not breathing until the heavy glass door slammed behind me.

I stopped in front of my dorm door and took a deep breath through my nose. Since I'd left, Paige had come back and put up our mini-whiteboard on the door and had written *Sasha & Paige's Room* in bubbly script with pink and purple dry-erase markers.

I hadn't told Paige anything all summer about the Jacob sitch, mostly because I hadn't wanted to think about it. But I was glad that we were rooming together again and I could finally talk about it. Paige was the best with boy advice and I knew she'd help me come up with a solution to the Jacob problem.

"Hey," I said, opening the door.

Paige, arms full of clothes, smiled at me. Her red-gold hair was in a half updo and she looked summery in a white cotton dress and silver flip-flops.

"Hi, fellow *eighth* grader," she said. Paige looked at my empty hands. "Forget about the Sweet Shoppe?"

I froze. "Oh. I'm sorry. I—my dad called and I got distracted and forgot. I'll go back later, promise."

Paige laid the pile of clothes on top of her plum-colored bedspread and waved her hand. "No big deal. We can go together later."

"Cool." I smiled at her and knelt in front of my suit-cases, unzipping the biggest one.

"We've got to decorate after we unpack and make some room," Paige said. "I've got the posters we bought in

Manhattan, you brought the new area rug, and I . . . have a surprise."

"Oooh," I said. "What'd you bring?"

Paige reached into a suitcase and pulled out a box. "Just surround sound for the TV. You know, so we can enjoy our Bennett Moore films a *little* bit more."

"And we're unpacking *why*?" I asked. "We should totally be watching his new flick right now!"

"After. It's our reward."

I mock-rolled my eyes at Paige and gave an exaggerated sigh. "Fiiiine." I started tossing clothes out of my suitcase and they landed in a heap on my bed. I zipped the suitcase shut and shoved it into the back of my closet. "One down!"

Paige gasped. "Sasha!" But she couldn't stop her laughter.

We raced through unpacking and the busier I became, the more I was able to shake off the weirdness of seeing Jacob, lying to Paige, and feeling guilty about Callie.

3

AND IN ONE CORNER
WE HAVE . . .

ON SUNDAY MORNING, I TOOK A SEAT ACROSS from Ms. Utz hoping I'd get out alive. She was—no joke—a wrestler on the weekends. Her office was decorated with championship belts and trophies.

"Did you have a good summer?" Ms. Utz asked, reaching to take the paper from me. She practically gave me a paper cut as she ripped it from my fingers. Like always, her hair was pulled into a severe bun and she looked as if she drank those chalky protein shakes for every meal. And snacks. And desserts.

"It was busy," I said. "I participated at a riding camp and spent the rest of the time at home. But I'm glad to be back."

As long as I can avoid Jacob twenty-four-seven, I thought.

Ms. Utz nodded and her giant fingers banged on the

keyboard as she checked to see what was available. Back home in Union, I wouldn't have had a choice of classes. But here, students had the privilege of choosing from certain subjects and difficulty levels. This year, I'd decided to challenge myself in my favorite subject—English—and had requested to take an advanced class.

"These courses look excellent, Sasha," Ms. Utz said. "I've added your name to rosters for advanced English, science, math, and history. You don't need PE because of riding, but you do need two electives. One has to be health and the other is up to you."

She looked back at her computer screen. "This year, we've added a few new courses. Do you need to see those or have you already decided?"

"I know already," I said. "I'd like to sign up for drama."

"Great choice. What inspired your decision?"

"Mr. Ramirez's film class. I loved learning about film, so theater sounds like fun." Totally true, but it wasn't the only reason why I'd picked the course.

"You want to become an actress?" Ms. Utz asked.

"Not really. I'd rather open a training stable one day. Film's more like a hobby."

Ms. Utz nodded. "Running a stable sounds like

something you'd enjoy, too, which is as important as anything."

With a click of the mouse, Ms. Utz's printer started whirring and she handed me my schedule.

"And you're set," she said. She tried to stand, but her knees caught under the desk. It tilted a couple of inches toward me and her giant mug of coffee almost tipped over. Liquid sloshed onto her oversize desktop calendar.

"Oops," she said. She got up and walked me to the door. "I'm confident you'll do great in these classes, Sasha. Come see me if you need to talk."

She patted my shoulder in what I'm sure was meant to be a gentle way, but it almost sent me flying through her office door.

"Thank you," I said. I left her office and started down the long hallway. I stared at my schedule, my eyes focused on the drama elective. I *did* love movies, and Mr. Ramirez's class had been my favorite last year. But I also needed at least one class where I knew I was safe from Jacob. I knew from our documentary project last year that he was pretty shy on camera—I had a feeling drama was the last course he would ever take.

Within seconds of leaving the administration meeting, beads of sweat collected over my lip and on my forehead. The summer air had turned superhumid and I felt my flatironed straight hair start to get wavy. I pulled it into a sloppy ponytail and eyed the Sweet Shoppe. I needed something cold.

"SASHA!"

Callie ran up the sidewalk toward me.

"CALLIE!" I called. I jammed my crumpled schedule into my back pocket and ran up to her. We hugged each other so hard that we almost toppled off the sidewalk and onto the grass. My uneasiness about seeing Callie for the first time since Jacob's confession vanished—all I saw was my best friend.

"Omigod, I missed you!" Callie said, grinning. The girl standing in front of me wasn't the old Callie Harper. The old Callie had just barely begun experimenting with makeup, only wore skirts on dates, and always chose comfort over fashion. This girl—New Callie—looked effortlessly cool in a royal blue pocket dress with spaghetti straps. She wore three skinny silver necklaces that I'd never seen before and tiny diamond studs sparkled in her ears.

"Me too! Summers suck for best friends who live so far apart."

Callie nodded and tucked a lock of raven-colored hair behind her ear. "Plus, we didn't even see each other yester-day. Do you have time to hang out now?"

"I was just going to get something icy from the Sweet Shoppe. Wanna come?"

"For sure." Callie fell into step beside me.

I loved this—us hanging out together. She was my best friend and we'd do anything for each other. That's why I'd made the decision over the summer to *never* tell her what Jacob had said to me. She liked him too much and I knew it would kill her to know about Jacob's feelings for me. By keeping the truth from Callie, I was protecting her. And that felt right.

I looked over at Callie, narrowing my eyes. "Did you get new makeup without me?" I asked in a teasing voice.

Callie laughed. "Maybe just a few things. You like it?"

"Like? Uh, love. You looked great before, but the new colors are fun. Very light and summery."

Callie looked older and more sophisticated—like thirteen and a half instead of twelve. Rosy blush complemented her caramel-colored skin and her eyelids shimmered with deep brown shadow. Her shiny lips kept the look fresh. She'd stepped up her game since she'd started dating Jacob.

We walked into the Sweet Shoppe and stood in front of the counter. "We *need* a sugar rush before tomorrow, right?" Callie asked with a knowing smile.

"Given," I said. "'Cause that's when the craziness starts."

"Mondays!" we said at the same time, then giggled.

The barista took our order and by the time she rang up our total, at least ten people had lined up behind us. We'd ordered almost one of everything.

"I think we got enough to get started," I said. I grabbed two of our four trays.

"But we'll see how it goes." We took the biggest empty table in the shop.

We spread out the treats and dug in. I went for mint chocolate chip ice cream first and Callie gulped her lemonade and strawberry slush.

"Did you get your schedule yet?" I asked Callie.

Nodding, she pulled it out of her shoulder bag. I dug mine out of my pocket. We moved a tray and spread the papers on the table, putting them side by side.

Callie ran her fingers down the list. "Awesome! This is the best schedule ever! We get to share a lot of classes."

"I know," I said. "It's going to be great."

"Drama's perfect for you," Callie said. "You'll, like, become a famous actor and give up horses."

"I'll stop riding Charm and will just run lines with him," I joked.

Callie shook her head. "I think Eric would be slightly devastated if you stopped riding. Just slightly."

"Possibly." I smiled at Callie.

"Have you seen him yet?" Callie asked. "You have to compare classes!"

"I saw him yesterday, but I'll e-mail him my schedule." I said. "I knew I missed him, but I didn't know how much till I saw him."

"Same thing with Jacob and me," Callie said. "I'm going to call him later and see what he got. We *better* have lots of classes together or I'll . . ."

"Challenge Utz to a wrestling match," I said, laughing. "When I saw Eric before my YENT meeting, he—" I stopped talking when I realized what I'd just said. "Sorry. I didn't mean to bring it up."

"Sasha, don't," Callie said. "You can talk about the YENT. I *want* you to. It's the biggest, most important thing that ever happened to you. You're my best friend— you know I'm happy for you."

"I know. I just don't want to make you sad by talking about it. If it ever bothers you, you'll tell me, right?"

Callie reached over the brownie plate and stuck out her pinky. "Promise."

We linked pinkies and giggled.

"Oh, *great*," someone said.

We looked up to see Julia Myer and Alison

Robb—Heather's BFFs—shaking their heads. Alison's wavy, sandy-colored locks were pinned into a loose twist and she wore an ubertrendy jean miniskirt and a lavender one-shoulder shirt. Julia's already superblond bob had highlights from the sun. Like Alison, she wore a cute mini and bubble-gum pink flip-flops.

"Nice to see you too," I said sweetly.

"Seriously?" Julia continued. "School hasn't even started yet and you guys are already doing your lame little BFF ritual at the Sweet Shoppe."

"Then what are *you* guys doing here?" Callie asked with a smirk.

"Getting cherry limeades and then . . ." Alison let her sentence trail off when Julia glared at her.

"We have other stuff to do besides sit here and consume our weight in sugar," Julia said. "You guys *could* be riding, you know."

"Did your parents let you ride at all over the summer?" Callie asked, her voice softening.

Alison shook her head. "I watched a trainer at my old stable ride Sunstruck," she said. "My parents wouldn't even let me ride him once."

"Mine either," Julia said. "So we just had the worst summers ever. Probably like yours, Callie. Sasha's the only one who actually got to ride. How nice for *you*." She glared at me when she said the last sentence.

"But," I started, "I—"

"Excuse me," Callie said, interrupting. "My summer was *great*. Don't come over to our table and be like that. It's not Sasha's fault that you guys cheated and got kicked off the team."

Julia glared at Callie. "Let's go," she said to Alison. "I don't know why we even bothered wasting our time."

"Some things never change," Callie said.

I nodded, pretending to agree. If only Callie knew *everything* had changed.

4

HELLO, EIGHTH GRADE!

BEEP! BEEP! BEEP!

"Nooo," Paige said, groaning. She rolled over and slapped the Hello Kitty alarm clock that was on the night-stand between our beds.

"We *just* went to sleep," I mumbled. I got up and flicked on our floor lamp. "Maybe since it *is* the first day of school, we'll get a break and the teachers won't make us do much."

Paige shook her head as she walked into the bath-room. "I'm not even going to bother justifying that with a response."

Sigh. She was right. Last year, teachers had given us tons of homework on the first day. But I'd been Union Sasha then—I hadn't known what to expect, had zero friends, and couldn't handle the workload. Canterwood Sasha had friends and an amazing boyfriend and she rode for the YENT. Eighth grade was going to be perfect . . . as soon as I figured out how to deal with Jacob.

Paige and I showered, did our hair, and got dressed. We slipped right into our old routine as though we'd never spent the summer away from Canterwood.

"Do I have to wear these?" I asked Paige, glancing down at my shoes. "I might hate myself later if I wear them and my feet start to hurt."

Paige laughed and eyed me. "The shoes have to stay. They make the outfit."

And they kind of did. I'd never worn them before, but they were black wedges that matched my heather gray shirt and black skirt.

I nodded. "True. I can deal. And the green shirt was def the right choice for you."

"Thanks!" Paige put tiny diamond studs in her ears. She'd picked a capped-sleeve hunter green shirt that made her fair skin look perfect and creamy. Plus, she'd paired it with skinny black jeans—jeans I planned to borrow (read: steal) next week.

I grabbed my backpack and checked my reflection one more time. Paige had given my hair tousled waves with her curling iron and she'd pulled her own hair into a sleek ponytail. We'd gone with the barely-there look for makeup—brown mascara, concealer, and lip gloss.

"It's weird not rushing off to the stable," I said. "We actually get to leave for class together."

Paige picked up her soft brown leather messenger bag and adjusted it over her shoulder. "Totally selfish—but I won't miss you getting up at six and clomping around in your boots."

I stuck out my bottom lip. "I tried to be quiet."

Paige rolled her eyes. "I was kidding, dork. I learned to sleep through it. Especially after listening to you snore every night."

Laughing, I pulled open the door and pushed her out into the hallway. The entire Winchester building had been given a makeover during the summer. The once bright yellow walls had been painted an eggshell white and the glossy wooden floors were shiny enough that I could practically see my reflection.

Paige and I walked by Livvie's office and she waved at us. She was a little neurotic—hello, she organized her paper-clip collection by size *and* color—but she was the best dorm monitor on campus. "Have a great first day, girls! Come see me if you need anything, okay?"

"We will," I promised.

Paige and I walked outside and started down the side-walk toward the science building. It was at the far end of campus by the tennis court.

"I'm glad we have our first class together," Paige said. "Think we'll know anyone else?"

"I don't know. I know Eric and Callie aren't in this class. With our luck, we'll probably have the Trio *and* Jasmine."

"But maybe we'll have . . ." Paige let her sentence trail off.

I playfully pushed her arm. "Maybe *you'll* have Ryan, you mean. Just say it."

Paige blushed. "Well, yeah. But we only IMed a little over the summer. That was it."

"A little? Every week is not 'a little'!"

"Okay, okay! We IMed a lot, but I don't even know if he really likes me. We just talked about general stuff."

"He likes you," I said. "I saw it at your *Teen Cuisine* party."

Teen Cuisine was the hottest show on The Food Network for Kids. Paige would never bring it up, but she hosted the show and was kind of a campus celebrity.

Paige smiled as we walked up the stairs and into the

English building. Canterwood's buildings looked more like an Ivy League campus than a middle school and high school. The two arched windows above the double doors flooded the marble hallway with light. Students hurried down the main hallway that split off into different corridors. Along the central hall, framed black-and-white photos of famous writers and authors who had graduated from Canterwood hung on the walls.

Paige took a purple folder out of her bag and consulted her schedule. "Room 302. So, third floor, obvi."

"Oooh, the special floor. I've never been up there," I said.

"Me neither. It's just for advanced classes."

We took the stairs and wandered down the hallway until we found the room. I opened the door and stopped, almost causing Paige to plow into my back.

"Whoaaa," I said. "*This* is our classroom?"

Eleven cozy-looking chairs were arranged in a circle around a square coffee table. Under the chairs and table, a plush burgundy rug made the vanilla-colored walls feel warm and cozy. We were the first ones there.

"If *all* advanced classes get rooms like these, I'm dropping my other classes and signing up for these," Paige said. "I'll just never sleep to keep up with the workload."

"I had Mr. Davidson last year and I can't believe he made us stay in a regular classroom when his eighth graders had *this*," I said.

The rest of the class, including Alison, trickled in and a guy I didn't recognize sat in the next-to-last empty seat as Mr. Davidson walked in.

"Welcome, everyone," he said. "For those of you who weren't in my class last year, my name is Mr. Davidson and I'll be your teacher for advanced eighth-grade English. As you can see, there are only ten of you. The setup may be a little different from what you're used to."

I looked around the circle as the other students nodded.

"This class will consist mostly of discussion. Yes, you will write papers, but it will mainly be a class open for dialogue. I hope you'll learn more debating each other about literature than dashing off a paper on Hemingway two hours before it's due.

"I want everyone to feel comfortable enough to express his or her opinion about whatever book we're reading," Mr. Davidson said. "That's why I chose this setting. I want each of us to come prepared to class every day ready to talk about what we've read. No one's opinion is dumb or wrong, so don't be afraid to speak."

Mr. Davidson ran a hand over his short blond hair. "But do not make the mistake of thinking this will be a class where you can show up and let everyone else talk. If you have not done the reading and cannot participate in intelligent discussion, you will be dismissed from my class. Understood?"

We nodded.

He lowered himself into his chair and looked at us. "To ease us into discussion, we'll spend the period introducing ourselves and getting to know one another. You'll tell me one thing about yourself, and name your favorite book. I'll start."

Everyone looked at him.

"So, as you already know, I'm Mr. Davidson. My favorite book is *The Call of the Wild*. I love dogs and on the weekends, my wife and I train a search-and-rescue dog that we sponsor."

"Really?" asked one of the girls. "That's so cool."

We all nodded. I never expected him to say anything like that.

Mr. Davidson turned to the girl sitting next to him.

"Hey, I'm Vanessa," she said.

And we kept moving around the room until it was Alison's turn.

"Hi, I'm Alison. My favorite book is actually a graphic novel—*The Black Cat*. I love it because it has a good story and because I, um, draw. I'm trying to become a better writer so I can have good stories for my illustrations."

"I haven't read many graphic novels, Alison, but perhaps you could recommend me a few of your favorites," Mr. Davidson said.

"Okay," Alison said, grinning. She scribbled a note in her folder. The more time I spent with Alison, the more I realized that I knew absolutely nothing about her. I'd seen a couple of her horse sketches, but I had no idea she wanted to write. I wondered if her graphic novels were about horses.

Mr. Davidson looked over at me, smiling.

I looked around at the group. "I'm Sasha. I've read *My Friend Flicka* only a hundred times. My mom had to buy me another copy because the pages started falling out. I'm on the riding team and spend most of my time at the stable."

"That's a wonderful book," Mr. Davidson said. "I read it several years ago and really enjoyed it."

Paige was up next.

"Hi," she said. "I'm Paige Parker and my favorite book is *Alice in Wonderland*. I read it after watching the Disney movie a zillion times when I was a kid. I love to cook and spend waaay too much time dreaming up new recipes that usually fail."

Everyone laughed. Paige could have told everyone that she was a TV star and gotten away with it because she was so nice, but she'd never do that.

Then, Mandy, Brad, Derek, Lee, and Aaron went. Paige and I traded smiles. This was the coolest class ever.

"I'm glad to know your favorite books," Mr. Davidson said. "All of your picks say something about you and none of your choices were even close to the same book. I think we're going to have a great class."

We smiled.

"Take a look at the syllabus," Mr. Davidson said. "Read the assigned chapters in our first book—*The Secret Garden*—and be prepared to discuss tomorrow. It's time for everyone to get to their next class."

Everyone looked at the clock. That was the fastest class ever! Paige and I walked out of the classroom together.

"That is *so* my favorite class," I said.

Paige giggled. "It's only the first one."

"Seriously? You think anything can top *that*?" I checked my schedule. "Not unless the Sweet Shoppe is catering our science class. Let's go."

We started for the science building. It was just a short walk down the hill.

"Sooo," Paige said. "I was looking at the calendar and there's something, like, special happening this week."

"Really?" I pretended to be confused. "Like what?"

"Your thirteenth birthday! That's the only benefit of school starting a week early—we get to celebrate together!"

I smiled. "That's def a benefit."

Paige whipped out her purple and white striped notebook. "Since your birthday's on Thursday and it's already Monday, it's way too late to plan a party on your actual birthday. I already texted Callie and we want to throw you a blowout party next Friday. Interested?"

I almost dropped my books. "Paige! Omigod! That's so sweet of you guys."

Paige wouldn't even look at me as she wrote in her notebook; she just nodded. "You'll have the best night ever."

We reached the science building, found our room, and took a couple of seats at one of the rows of long tables. Two giant whiteboards were at the front of the class and the teacher's desk was off in the corner. It was covered with geeky gadgets—like the swinging magnetic balls, orbs with electricity, and a vase of sand art.

As I took out my book, I couldn't stop watching the door. Jacob was going to be in one of my classes—I just had a feeling. I'd take the Trio *and* Jasmine in class over him.

I looked at Paige out of the corner of my eye as she took out a clean sheet of paper and got ready to take notes. I had to tell her about Jacob. She was my close friend and I needed someone to talk to or I'd go crazy. Even though Paige didn't have a boyfriend, she gave the best guy advice. If she ever quit hosting *Teen Cuisine*, she could totally write an advice column for *Fifteen*.

"Paige," I said, leaning over. "After class, I want to talk to—"

I stopped talking when my eyes flickered to the guy walking through the door.

Ryan. Paige's crush. He was *so* her type. Dark brown hair, intense eyes, and fair skin. Not a football player, but he definitely spent time in the gym.

Paige blushed, ducking her head, then glanced back up. Ryan scanned the classroom for an empty seat and he saw Paige. He smiled and walked toward us. There was a seat at the table in front of us.

Take it! Sit there! I tried to will Ryan through ESP.

He dropped his backpack onto the floor and slid into the right chair. He turned around, flashing dimples.

"Hey, guys," he said.

I smiled back, keeping one eye on Paige to make sure she didn't decide to bolt for the door or something. "Hi, Ryan. Did you have a good summer?"

"Totally," Ryan said. "I spent most of it at my brother's house on the Cape. I went surfing every day and rode his Jet Ski. It was awesome."

I looked at Paige, waiting for her to jump in and start talking. She'd been awkward around Ryan before summer break, but I'd hoped the IMing would have made her more comfortable around him. Her face, however, was bright pink and she kept her eyes on the paper on her desk.

"You hear anything about this class?" Ryan asked, directing his question to Paige.

Paige looked up and played with her pen. "Um, I read on FaceSpace that the teacher gives a lot of homework, but nothing too bad. And Sasha had her last year and the teacher was kind of tough."

"You need to friend me," Ryan said. "We chatted all summer and I don't even think we're friends. That's kind of wrong."

"So wrong," Paige said, smiling.

I hid my own grin. They'd be dating in no time. And Ryan seemed like a good guy, so I wasn't worried about

Paige. Ryan turned around when our teacher, Ms. Peterson, walked into the classroom.

"Hey, what were you about to say before?" Paige whispered.

"Nothing—tell you later," I said.

"Welcome, class," Ms. Peterson said, tucking a lock of her chin-length dark hair behind her ear. "Let's start with attendance and then we'll go through the syllabus. I want to make sure everyone is aware of the deadlines for important papers and projects from the beginning."

She was going to be tough—she was last year. Ms. Peterson took attendance and then passed out papers to all of us.

Her syllabus was twenty-four pages long, in size-ten font and with tiny margins.

"First," Ms. Peterson said. "Let me say that I do not tolerate lateness. If you're late—don't bother coming to my class. The same rule applies with papers and projects—if you miss a deadline, it's an automatic zero. No makeups."

Everyone in the class was still. I surreptitiously capped my pink pen and traded it for a blue one. I had a feeling my paper would come back to me ripped into pieces if I turned it in with pink ink.

As I listened to Ms. Peterson, I glanced over at Paige's desk. She was drawing a tiny heart on the inside of her folder. *P & R* was written inside the heart.

Suddenly, I knew I couldn't tell Paige about Jacob. Not now. Not when she was just starting to like a guy herself. The focus should be on her for once—not my ever-present boy drama. I wasn't going to take away from her crush on Ryan. I had to handle this on my own.

My phone buzzed and I opened it to find a text from Callie. *Eric and I r in the same sci class. Cool, huh?*

Awesome! I wrote back. Ms. Peterson shifted toward my side of the room and I shoved my phone under my leg.

But maybe it wasn't so awesome. My best friend and boyfriend were in the same class—alone—every day. What if they somehow figured out that Jacob and I were acting weird and realized something had happened between us?

I caught Paige looking at me and I smiled at her. Suddenly, I was glad I'd signed up for theater. I had a feeling the acting lessons were going to come in handy.

5

LESSON ONE

BY THE TIME I WALKED TO THE STABLE FOR
my first YENT lesson, I was exhausted. I'd spent my
lunch period in the bathroom, sitting in a locked stall and
working on homework. I'd been too nervous about seeing
Jacob at lunch to go. Thankfully, Callie had bought my
excuse that I had to run to the admin office before my
next class.

I passed Black Jack's stall at the stable. Callie's Morab
gelding was snoozing in the back of his stall. I stopped and
looked at him. Charm and I had both lost a teammate.

Jack walked up to me and put his head over the stall
door. I scratched under his forelock, then rubbed his
cheek. I'd never be able to make it up to Callie for what
had happened. It wasn't my fault that Jacob had started

liking me again, I knew that, but I still felt bad. If Jacob hadn't been acting so weird, maybe Callie and I would be grooming our horses for practice right now. I'd *never* had a lesson without Callie.

Ever.

"See you later, boy," I told Jack. I left him, grabbed Charm's tack, and went to his stall.

"Hi, guy," I said to him.

I led him out and started grooming him in the cross-ties. My mind had just begun to wander when I heard hoofbeats clattering down the aisle. I looked up from brushing Charm's flank and Heather was glaring at me, holding a tacked-up Aristocrat.

"Do you think Mr. Conner will wait for you to show up, or what?" Heather asked.

"What?" I checked the giant wall clock near the grain room. "Omigod! We have to be there in two minutes! I totally spaced."

I dropped Charm's body brush and scrambled to grab his tack from on top of the trunk in front of his stall.

"Obvi," Heather said. She looked over her shoulder, then let go of Aristocrat's reins. "Give me Charm's bridle." She held out her hand to me.

I tried to keep my mouth from falling open. "Thanks."

"Oh, don't look at me like that. I'll deny it if you *ever* tell anyone I helped you. And I'm only doing it because I don't want the *real* Canterwood riders to ever look bad. No matter what Mr. Conner says, Jas is *not* part of our team."

I didn't dare argue with her. Heather and Jas would never stop hating each other. No matter how long Jasmine was at Canterwood, Heather would always see her as an outsider.

Heather bridled Charm while I saddled him. I put on my helmet and we led both horses toward the exit.

"Really, thanks," I said.

Heather rolled her eyes and walked faster. "You can stop talking to me now."

I laughed under my breath and stopped Charm a few feet out of the stable. The sun hid behind fat, puffy clouds and a slight breeze tugged at Charm's mane. Heather and I mounted and let the horses walk toward the arena.

At the far end, Jasmine warmed up Phoenix. The gray gelding, sweating in the heat, moved perfectly under Jasmine. They looked even better than they had at YENT camp. I let Charm into a slow trot, forcing myself to focus and not worry about Jasmine and Heather.

But I couldn't stop sneaking glances at them. My old

insecurities about my riding abilities had hit me full force at YENT camp this summer. I'd felt alone without Callie in the arena. That anxiety was hitting me again and making my chest feel white-hot with panic.

Charm jerked his head and sidestepped. I pressed my right boot into him and moved him back to the arena wall. "Cool it," I murmured to him. He strained against the reins, wanting to trot faster. I held him back and didn't let him out. This was just a warm-up.

Mr. Conner walked into the arena and motioned for us to line up in front of him. I angled Charm between Aristocrat and Phoenix.

"Hi, girls," he said. "I don't want to waste time talking since you know how my lessons work."

Charm, mouthing the bit, fidgeted and sidestepped—again—causing my boot to bump against Heather's.

"Sorry!" I said. My face, already flushed from the heat, turned what I was sure about five different shades of red as I sat deeper in the saddle and tried to quiet Charm with my hands.

"Go ahead and move out to the wall at a walk," Mr. Conner said.

Jasmine, Heather, and I turned the horses away from Mr. Conner.

"Wow, Sasha," Jasmine said, lowering her voice. "You benefitted so much from YENT camp—it's just ridic. I'm jealous."

I ignored her and tried to look as if I didn't care.

But I did. And Jas knew it.

"Starting today," Mr. Conner called. "I'm going to be treating some of the lessons as equitation practices."

I didn't know whether to cheer or freak out.

"Remember that for equitation," Mr. Conner continued. "My focus is on *you*, not your horse. I will be watching your hands, seats, and legs, and will comment on your horse only if he exhibits extraordinarily bad behavior."

The good: Mr. Conner wouldn't hold it against me that Charm was a little off today.

The bad: My focus was on controlling Charm and not on my posture.

I took a breath, trying to relax. Charm was feeling my tension—that was usually the only reason why he ever acted up.

"Sitting trot," Mr. Conner said.

Charm bounded forward from a light tap of my heels. He jerked on my hands and I fought to regain my posture before Mr. Conner saw.

"Sasha," he called out. "Your body needs to be just a

few degrees in front of vertical. Sit back a little."

I pushed my shoulders back, knowing I looked stiff instead of relaxed like Mr. Conner wanted, but I couldn't focus on myself when I had to concentrate on Charm, too.

"Halt," Mr. Conner instructed.

Within a few strides, we'd brought our horses to smooth stops.

"Back up five strides," Mr. Conner said.

We did and Charm snuck his muzzle in the air instead of tucking his chin. Phoenix and Aristocrat backed up without hesitation. I chewed on the inside of my lip, trying not to cry. My first lesson on the Canterwood YENT was a disaster.

"Halt, then move into a trot for a lap," Mr. Conner said.

We stopped our horses, then urged them into trots. Charm mouthed the bit—playing with it with his tongue. His ears pointed forward and he didn't pay attention to me. I closed my fingers around the reins, trying to get his focus. He flicked an ear back at me, then pointed them forward again.

"Canter," Mr. Conner said.

Charm shot forward—taking Mr. Conner's command as a verbal cue. Charm pulled me forward and the reins slipped through my fingers.

"Sasha, watch your shoulders," Mr. Conner called. "Pull Charm back to a trot, then tell him to canter. He should not have started on my cue instead of yours."

My face burned.

I slowed Charm to a trot and he shook his head, tossing his mane. I held him back as he watched Aristocrat and Phoenix canter ahead of him. Charm *hated* it when other horses were moving faster in front of him. But I didn't give in—I made him trot even though he swished his tail hard from side to side. After a few more strides, he started to settle and respond to me. I relaxed my fingers on the reins and gave him more. He broke into an even canter and I tried to shake off my nerves.

By the end of class, my arms were sore from fighting with Charm and I was exhausted from worrying about how I looked next to Heather and Jasmine. My T-shirt was soaked from sweat, and strands of hair that had escaped from my ponytail were plastered to the back of my neck.

"Good work, girls," Mr. Conner said. "Take extra time to care for your horses because of the heat—make sure you give them small sips of water while you cool them out. See you tomorrow."

We dismounted and I walked Charm in front of Heather

and Jas. We got inside the stable and I walked him up and down the side aisle, both of us still sweating.

"I'm sorry," I whispered to him. "That was my fault—not yours."

Charm rubbed his cheek against my arm and turned his head to look at me. He was trying to tell me something. I hugged his neck. "You're right—I wasn't alone in the arena. I've got you, boy."

It took over half an hour of walking before he was cool. I led him to the wash stall and rinsed the dried-up sweat from his coat. Charm sighed happily as the cool water ran over his back. After he was clean, I dried him with a couple of towels, then put him in his stall.

I started out of the stable and groaned to myself when I saw Rachel carrying a water bucket down the aisle. The seventh grader had an obvious crush on Eric and she wasn't shy about showing it. She was petite with light brown hair and natural reddish highlights. I noticed she'd switched from glasses to contacts over the summer.

"Good summer?" Rachel asked, stopping in the aisle. She looked perfect—not at all sweaty in the heat.

"Awesome. You?"

"Pretty cool. I went on an overnight trail ride with my friends. Sleeping outside kinda sucked, but the rest was fun." Rachel shifted the green bucket from one hand to the other. "Bet it was hard to be separated from Eric all summer. And now you guys don't even have lessons together anymore." She stuck out her bottom lip.

I shrugged. "It's cool. We iChatted all summer and now we can see each other whenever we want."

Rachel smiled. "Oooh, good. Mr. Conner said the intermediate team could watch an advanced lesson once a week and everyone's, like, so excited to go."

You are because you get to watch my boyfriend! I thought. But I kept a nonchalant expression on my face. I still couldn't forget that I'd overheard Rachel and her friends talking last spring about how hot Eric was.

"That's great. I'm sure you'll learn a lot."

I walked away from her, glad that I'd been cool. I had no reason to worry about Eric. Rachel could go to *every* one of Eric's lessons if she wanted—he'd never be interested in her.

6

STALKER, MUCH?

WHEN IT WAS TIME FOR LUNCH ON TUESDAY, I went to the salad bar, skipping the hot lunch line, and grabbed a plateful of fruits and veggies. The most eventful class of yesterday? History. Both Eric and Jacob were in my class. They'd sat at opposite ends of the room and hadn't looked at each other once. At least our teacher, Mr. Spellman, had been awesome enough to let us go after taking attendance and going through the syllabus. He'd understood that we'd all felt overwhelmed after the first day and needed a few minutes to breathe.

I took a seat at the table I usually shared with my friends. We all kind of rotated around the caf since we had friends in different groups. No one else was here yet, so I speared a forkful of lettuce and started eating.

A tray clattered onto the space in front of me and I looked up at Jacob.

I dropped my fork and stared at him for a second. "What are you doing?"

"Sasha, c'mon, would you talk to me, please?" Jacob sat down and, instinctively, I scooted back a few inches.

"No, I don't want Callie or Eric to see us talking. They'll be here any second."

Jacob shook his head. "Callie's science class ran late—some kind of lab thing. And since Eric's in that class . . ."

"Okay, fine, whatever. But you still can't sit here. Please just go."

Jacob stared at me for a second, looking as if he wanted to argue. But a look—hurt, maybe—flashed across his face. He gave me a half smile. "Okay. Sorry."

He picked up his tray and I watched him walk away, his shoulders slumped a little. I hadn't meant to hurt his feelings, but I also couldn't be worrying every two seconds about running into him. I'd stressed all summer over what he'd told me and it was a thousand times harder now that I was on campus and had to actually see him. Suddenly, I wasn't so hungry. I left the caf and took my time walking to math class. My phone buzzed and I opened it to see a text from Eric.

Sry I missed lunch! :(

No prob. Skipped anyway.

I regretted the text as soon as I sent it. I hadn't meant to lie. But I was feeling so on edge about Jacob, it had just slipped out.

In math, Callie slid into the seat across from me. She smiled in my direction, but didn't take her eyes off her BlackBerry as she texted.

"Should I leave you two alone?" I joked.

"Sorry," Callie said, putting it down on her desk. "I've been texting Jacob, but he hasn't written me back yet."

I stared down at my desk. "Oh, he's prob just running to his next class or something. You know how things are still crazy and it's only the second day and he'll totally text you back because, you know, he's *your* boyfriend. So . . ." *Stop rambling!* I shouted to myself. I closed my mouth.

Callie nodded, straightening her sky blue T-shirt. "I know. You're right." She laughed. "Ugh, I can't turn into one of *those* girlfriends who thinks her boyfriend's up to something if he doesn't respond to her in five seconds."

"You're not. Trust me."

Yeah, trust me after I've been keeping a giant secret from you.

We got out our math notebooks. I'd been up past lights-out just to finish all of my homework. I was probably going to have to get up at the same time I used to last year for lessons just to keep up with homework and riding.

"Oh!" Callie said, turning to me. "I didn't even get to ask you about your lesson yesterday! How was it?"

I froze—unsure what to say. Did I tell her the truth that I'd been a mess? Or would she think I was being ungrateful since I'd gotten on the YENT and she hadn't?

"It was tough," I said, deciding not to lie. "I felt intimated up against Heather and Jasmine. It was weird without you there and I was tense, which made Charm nervous."

Callie winced. "Sorry it was hard. But it was just the first class. It'll get better. You know you're just as good as they are—don't let Jas freak you out. She does that on purpose."

"I know, you're right."

Callie munched on a potato chip. "Yesterday was weird for me, too. I was sad that we weren't in the same class. It's not as fun without you!"

I stared down at my plate. Here Callie was telling me how much she missed me and I was hiding a huge secret about her boyfriend. *But you're keeping Callie and Jacob together,* I reminded myself. Jacob made Callie happy. If I told her the truth, she'd be crushed.

***

At my riding lesson, I walked to the indoor arena sans Charm. Mr. Conner had e-mailed the YENT team this morning and had told us to come without our horses.

I stood by Heather, who, like me, was dressed in boots and breeches.

"What's going on?" I asked.

She shrugged. "No clue. I hope nothing's wrong. I know *I* didn't do anything. Did you?"

"No! Maybe—" I stopped talking when Jas walked in. I'd been about to say that maybe Jas had done something. But Mr. Conner walked in right behind her, leading three stable horses. We all looked at one another.

"Hi, girls," Mr. Conner said, smiling at us. "I'm going to give each of you a new horse for this lesson."

He walked to Heather and handed her the reins of a gray gelding. Jas got a blue roan and Mr. Conner gave me a dun. I patted my horse's shoulder and looked at Mr. Conner.

"Go ahead and mount," he said.

We mounted and I let out my stirrups a notch.

"I've said before that I want to focus on you, the riders, and not so much your horses. A great rider is able to get the best out of her mount—no matter what horse she might be riding." Mr. Conner looked back and forth among all of us. "Riders on the Olympics often train with at least two horses in case one becomes injured. So, I want you all to ride new horses today. Over the year, you'll continue to ride different horses."

I raised my hand and Mr. Conner nodded at me. "What are the horses' names?"

Mr. Conner smiled. "Of course. You're riding Knox, Jas has Summer, and Heather's riding Perry. Walk and trot them for a few minutes to get them warmed up and get a feel for how they handle."

I walked and trotted Knox for a couple of laps and while his stride wasn't as smooth as Charm's, he was a great horse. He listened to me and I could just tell that he wanted to please his rider.

Jas looked comfortable on Summer and Heather had no problem with Perry.

"Good," Mr. Conner said. "Let's do a few basic exercises, then we'll try something a little more difficult."

Knox didn't falter once through the next twenty minutes of exercises. I fell more in love with him every second. He was one of the sweetest horses I'd ever ridden.

"Cross over the center and reverse directions," Mr. Conner said.

I trotted Knox to the center of the arena and Heather, Jas, and I started trotting the horses in the opposite direction. Knox could have developed bad habits from being ridden by dozens of riders because of his career as a school horse. But instead, he responded to every command in a second and never questioned me.

Mr. Conner worked us for another half hour before dismissing us. I dismounted and handed Knox's reins to Mike—my fave groom. I hugged Knox's neck and made a mental note to take him a carrot later.

"Thanks," I said.

"Sure thing." Mike smiled and led Knox out of the arena.

I walked to Charm's stall to hug him good night. He leaned into me before his gaze shifted back to his hay net. Then, he craned his neck back to me and sniffed my shirt.

"What, boy?" I asked.

Charm smelled me again. "Oh! You probably smell Knox." I smiled. "I rode him because I *had* to. I would have much rather ridden you—you know that."

Charm eyed me, then nudged my arm with his head. "So we're okay, huh?" I asked. I hugged him again and he wandered over to his hay net.

I latched his stall shut and thought about today's lesson. I'd been able to relax instead of worrying about what Jas and Heather were doing. It had made *all* of the difference and I realized that's what I had to do—block them out.

I started out of the stable, glad Eric wasn't here to see me. I was a sweaty mess. Bits of hay were stuck to my old black breeches—the ones with holes in the knees—and my boots were covered in arena dust.

"Sasha!" A fake cheery voice called me from behind.

I turned and saw the Belles. Violet, Brianna, and Georgia—three ninth graders who thought they ruled the stable—walked my way. I brushed my hair off my forehead and folded my arms.

"What?" I asked.

Violet and her friends had tried to initiate Callie, the Trio, and me into their circle. We'd met them at the stable at midnight where they had dared us to ride our horses across campus. Heather and I had refused, but Callie, Julia, and Alison had agreed to do the dare. Before they could start, we'd all been caught by Mr. Conner. All of us were temporarily banned from riding and even though it had all been their idea, I had a feeling they hadn't let it go. To make things even worse, none of the Belles had been extended invites to try out for the YENT.

"How was your summer?" Violet asked.

"Oh, you know," I said, slowly. "YENT camp was amazing. Too bad you weren't there."

For a second, I felt a flash of guilt. My snarky comment sounded just like something Heather would say. But those girls deserved it.

Brianna stepped closer, her eyes on me. "Who wanted to spend all summer riding, anyway? We actually have lives. And whatever—we can still make the YENT at the next tryouts."

Georgia smirked. "BTW, did you check your *e-mail* much this summer?"

My hands clenched at my sides. Georgia Drake, the headmistress's daughter, had somehow used her mom's computer to hack into my e-mail account. She'd been the one who passed an e-mail to Violet that had started this whole mess in the first place. I'd written the e-mail *pre*-Eric and *pre*-Jacob-and-Callie, confessing I still had feelings for Jacob. But he never got it. Until, that is, right before the end of school while I was happy with Eric, and Callie and Jacob were together.

I started to reply to Georgia, but Jasmine sidled up next to the Belles and the older girls enveloped her in their group. I didn't know if Brianna, Georgia, and Violet trusted Jasmine enough to tell her what they'd done with the e-mail, but I definitely wasn't about to bring it up if Jasmine didn't already know.

"I've got to go," I said.

"Like always," Jas taunted behind my back. "Sasha Silver just walks away."

Ignoring Jasmine's comment, I walked around them and left the stable. There wasn't room in my brain for the Belles and their nasty tricks.

7

SASHA STARBUCKS

AT BREAKFAST THE NEXT MORNING, PAIGE AND I swiped our usual table. Paige eyed the cappuccino beside my plate of pancakes.

"What's with that, Starbucks?" she asked. "You never drink coffee in the morning."

I sipped the drink. "I know, but this week is insane. I think I'll fall asleep by history class if I don't have caffeine."

"Okay, but only because I don't want to be known as the BFF of the girl who drooled on her desk," Paige said, smiling.

"Oh, glad to know *that* was your reason."

We giggled and I sipped my coffee, waiting for the caffeine to kick in. I'd stayed up last night after Paige had gone to bed to work on a reading assignment for English. Teachers were already piling on the homework, but the work wasn't the problem—my concentration was. I kept going back and forth about confessing to Paige about the Jacob sitch. It was weird not to tell Paige everything—she and Callie were my BFFs. But I knew I had to keep this to myself.

I was drizzling (read: pouring) syrup onto my pancakes when Eric took a chair next to Paige and across from me.

Just looking at him made me need a little less coffee. He'd paired a vintage-y blue T-shirt with jeans and he still looked sleepy. Adorable.

"Pancakes, sure. But coffee?" he asked, smiling at me. "You okay?"

"Totally fine," I said. "Just needed a jolt for today."

His own tray had bacon, scrambled eggs, toast, and a glass of OJ. I leaned over and speared some eggs onto my fork, grinning at Eric's expression.

He retaliated by slicing off a bit of pancake with his fork and stuffing it into his mouth.

"You guys should just trade already," Paige said, laughing.

I looked over Paige's and Eric's shoulders and saw

Callie and Jacob walk into the caf holding hands. Callie looked totally adorable—she was wearing a black skirt, red ballet flats, and white boyfriend T-shirt. I couldn't get over her new look. She must have read a lot of *Teen Fashion* over the summer.

Callie waved at me and I smiled back.

She would have been at YENT camp, not reading fashion mags if you and Jacob hadn't messed up, I thought to myself.

I glued my eyes to my food and nodded, pretending to listen, as Paige and Eric talked about the possessed squirrel they were sure had claimed the best bench by the fountain.

"And that annoying thing totally started, like, chattering at this girl in my class when she walked by the bench," Paige said. "She . . ."

I zoned out again—not able to stop myself from watching Callie and Jacob.

They sat a few tables away, Callie's back to me. She was talking, laughing, and gesturing with her hands. Jacob, nodding, ate his bacon, egg, and cheese sandwich. His hair fell in front of one eye and he reached up to swipe it out of the way. He looked about as engaged in whatever Callie was saying as I was in Eric's and Paige's conversation. His eyes shifted away from Callie to me.

We held each other's gaze across the cafeteria. I couldn't even breathe. It was *Jacob*. He was with Callie—not me. That's what I'd wanted. And I was beyond happy with Eric. I was probably only paying attention to Jacob because I was nervous that he kept trying to talk to me every five minutes.

"Sasha?"

"What?" I ripped my eyes away from Jacob and looked at Paige.

She stuck out her tongue at me, teasingly. "Pay attention! Talking about the psycho squirrel is superimportant."

"Yeah, it's *super*important." I laughed. And for the rest of breakfast, I listened to Paige and Eric debate the squirrel's mental state and made sure I didn't even glance in Jacob's and Callie's direction.

It was almost seven when I finished my lesson and cooled Charm. Callie had texted me during math to see if I wanted to groom the horses together, so I hadn't brushed Charm after our lesson had ended. He was in crossties while I mucked out his stall.

I looked up when I heard footsteps stop outside the stall. Alison stood there and gave me a half smile. She was so much nicer when she wasn't with Julia.

"Hey," I said. "What's up?"

"Just came to see Sunstruck," Alison said. She played with the end of her loose French braid. "I try to spend more time with him now that I can't ride."

"How is he?" I asked.

Alison leaned against the doorway of Charm's stall. "Fine. I mean, I'm watching him for loss of muscle tone, but Mike's riding him at least every other day."

"You know," I said, leaning the pitchfork against the stall wall, "I read an article about hand-walking horses. You could take Sunstruck over the trails and jog with him. If you worked him up and down the hills, he'd stay in shape."

Alison smiled. "That's a good idea."

Alison turned to go, but stopped short. "Thanks, really. I'm going to talk to Mr. Conner about that."

"Good," I said. "Let me know how it goes. Maybe we can walk Charm and Sunstruck together sometime."

"Yeah," Alison nodded. "Maybe we can."

I'd just finished mucking Charm's stall when Callie appeared with Jack in tow.

"Hey! Want to tie them up by the pasture?" Callie asked. "It's nice out for once."

"Let's."

We grabbed our tack boxes and led Charm and Jack side by side down the aisle.

"We haven't had time to hang out at *all*," Callie said. "It's just wrong."

"I know. We're BFFs. It's a rule that we have to see each other more."

The sun was just starting to set as we reached the side pasture and tied the horses' lead lines to the pasture rail. I loved the campus this time of day—it looked softened by the fading light and it felt less crazy, less intimidating than usual.

"Paige was telling me about Ryan," Callie said. "She's so shy about him—I'm not used to seeing her like that."

I grabbed a dandy brush. "I know! It's so cute—she's a mess around him. Paige gives the best guy advice, but she's *so* nervous around Ryan," I said. "She really likes him a lot."

"We have to help her," Callie said, combing Jack's tail.

"I'll probably try to talk her into asking him out if he doesn't ask her soon. She should go for it. Why wait for him?"

Callie nodded. "Totally." She went back to grooming for a few minutes before looking at me. "I know exactly how we can get them together!"

"How?" I bent down to brush Charm's right foreleg.

"We just said that we haven't had much time to hang out, so why don't we *all* go out? Like a group date—very casual. You and Eric, Jacob and I, and Paige and Ryan."

I stopped in mid-brush stroke. "Uh—"

"It's perfect!" Callie said, practically bouncing up and down. "We can go to The Slice or something and it'll be a no-pressure thing for Paige to invite Ryan to."

I was glad Callie couldn't see my face behind Charm's leg. This was the worst idea *ever*! Eric and Jacob hated each other. I didn't want to be around Jacob. Paige knew nothing about what was going on and neither did Callie. All of us together was the last thing I wanted!

"It would be fun," I said slowly. "But . . . wouldn't things be a little uncomfortable between Jacob and Eric? They really don't like each other."

Callie dropped Jack's comb in her tack box and picked up a body brush. "I think they'll be cool. Jacob knows it's important to me that you and I get to hang out and you know Eric thinks the same. If they really care about us, they'll just deal."

I started to argue, but Callie's smile made me stop. She really wanted us to all go out. After all I'd done to her— everything she didn't know about—she deserved to have what she wanted.

"Okay," I said, forcing a grin. "We'll do it. But only if Paige wants to. I don't want to freak her out or anything."

"Deal. Ask her tonight. We'll plan for Friday!"

Callie didn't stop talking about our group date until we went off to our separate dorms an hour later.

When I got to my room, Paige was working at her desk. "Have fun with Callie?" she asked. I'd texted her earlier to say I was staying late at the stable.

"So much fun," I said. "And Callie had an idea that I'm supposed to run by you. But you can totally say no and I'd understand if you did." I kept rambling. "I told her you'd probably say no and she would completely get it."

Paige put down her pen, tilting her head a little. "What idea?"

I crossed my fingers that Paige wouldn't want to go. "Callie wants us all to go out on a group date to The Slice. Jacob. Eric. Me. Callie. You." I paused. "And Ryan."

Paige looked down at her open math book. She was going to say no. There's no way she'd—

"Okay," she said, jumping up from her seat. "I'll ask! I'll just e-mail him and be like, 'A bunch of us are going out. Come if you want.' Right?"

I blinked. "Riiight. Yeah. Do that."

I sat on my bed, not knowing what else to say. I was

torn. Ryan would definitely say yes and Paige would be thrilled. But the idea of Jacob, Callie, and Eric all together made my head pound.

"This is sooo awesome!" Paige said, grabbing my hand and pulling me up. She dragged me over to her laptop on her desk. "C'mon. Help me figure out what to say."

"Okay." I smiled for real. I loved seeing her this happy. Being uncomfortable for a couple of hours was worth it.

Paige and I shared her desk chair and she quickly closed a file that said *S's Bday*.

"Oooh! Show me!" I said, elbowing her.

Paige laughed. "No way. The details are super top secret."

"But tomorrow's my real birthday," I said, sticking out my lip in a pretend pout. "So, don't you feel that it would be, like, an early present to show me?"

"Nope. Guilt won't work, Sasha Silver. Puh-lease."

We giggled and I gave an exaggerated sigh. "Fiiine. Let's get Ryan to come out with us already."

We spent the next hour going over every word in the two line e-mail to Ryan.

"Is it really ready?" Paige asked. She looked back and forth from the computer to me.

"Send. It."

"One more read. Okay. 'Hey Ryan, a bunch of my friends and I are going to The Slice on Friday. Text or e-mail me if you want to come.'"

"It's perfect. Now hit send!" I said, laughing.

"But wait!" Paige said. "How do I sign it? 'Your friend, Paige' is lame."

I leaned over and typed ~*Paige*. "There. Done. Do it."

Paige closed her eyes and pressed send. I looked at Paige's hopeful smile and decided Callie's idea might not have been too awful. *One* night out wouldn't kill anyone.

8

BIRTHDAY GIRL

"HAPPY REAL BIRTHDAY!" PAIGE SAID, WAKING me the next morning. She sat cross-legged at the end of my bed. She was wearing my pink T-shirt emblazoned with a silver rhinestone heart.

I sat up, blinking and trying to tame my bed head. "Thanks! Do I look older? I feel older."

Paige nodded. "You look *so* much older. Definitely thirteen."

"Maybe fourteen with eyeliner?" I asked hopefully.

"Don't push it." Paige laughed.

Someone knocked on the door and Paige got up to answer it.

"Hey, birthday girl!" Callie said, stepping inside. She was carrying two giant bags from the Sweet Shoppe. She was dressed in yoga pants and a hoodie, her hair in a messy ponytail and she hadn't put on makeup yet.

"Cal! What are you doing here?"

Callie stepped inside and put the bags on my desk. Both she and Paige smiled at me.

"It's your birthday! Duh," Callie said, shaking her head.

"But, guys! You're already throwing me a party. That's waaay more than enough," I said.

Callie and Paige rolled their eyes.

"Get over here and look in the bag," Paige said. "You know you want to."

Grinning, I hopped out of bed. "Well, if you insist . . ."

We opened the bags and inside was a variety of scones, muffins, fruit salads, and pastries. There were also containers of cranberry and orange juice.

"Wow, this is amazing! Thank you!" I said.

Paige reached into her closet and pulled out a bag. She produced pink plastic plates and flatware.

"We wanted to have a best-friend breakfast just for the girls this morning," Paige said. "You get to pick first."

We loaded our plates and sat in the middle of the floor. I'd chosen two chocolate croissants and a blueberry scone. Yum.

"Raise your cups," Callie said.

We all did, smiling at one another.

"To Sasha on her official birthday," Callie continued, her brown eyes warm. "The best friend Paige and I could ever have. We hope you have the most amazing birthday ever!"

"Not just today, but also at your actual party!" Paige added, laughing.

"Cheers to that. Thanks, guys." We touched our juice containers together and giggled. We started eating and I glanced up at them for a second. Even though I was keeping secrets from both of them, I was more convinced than ever that I was doing the right thing.

Half an hour later, Callie left and Paige started to get ready for class.

"Sooo," Paige said. "I have an early sort-of present for you."

I put down my blush brush. "Really? What?"

Paige looked at me from the mirror as she flatironed her hair. "Fall break is, like, three-ish weeks away. I'd love for you to come stay with me in New York. If you want, of course."

I bounced up and down. "Really?! Omigod, I'd love to!

I loved New York so much and we didn't even get through half of the things on our to-do list."

"Exactly." Paige grinned. "Ask your parents. Mine already said yes."

"I totally will," I said. "Now we have something awesome to look forward to when we're up till one studying."

"For sure."

We finished getting ready and Paige shouldered her bag, looking at me.

"You go ahead," I told Paige. "I want to check my e-mail. I'll see you in class."

"Okay," Paige nodded. "See you there."

I stuffed the rest of my books into my backpack, waiting until Paige's footsteps disappeared down the hallway before I sank into my desk chair. I played with a charm on my bracelet—a good luck horseshoe that Eric had given me on our first date. I closed my eyes and took a deep breath. I'd been at school barely six days and I was already exhausted from classes, riding . . . and worrying. But I reminded myself that I was also keeping the secret to save my relationship with Eric. If he found out what I was hiding from him about Jacob, he'd be furious.

I opened my eyes and flipped open my sleeping laptop.

I pulled up my e-mail and saw *two new messages*. I clicked and my shoulders slumped a little when I saw the subjects— *You've won a million dollars in the lottery!!* and *Come find Mr. Right at DateGirl.com.*

I slammed the lid closed. I'd thought maybe . . . no. I wasn't going there.

"Ugh!" I said out loud. *I* was the problem! If I told Jacob to stay away from me, then why was I disappointed when he didn't e-mail to say happy birthday?

I jumped up, my left knee slamming into the desk. "Ow!" I rubbed my knee and yanked my backpack off my bed. I jerked the door shut behind me, probably hard enough to rattle every window in Winchester.

What was my problem?! I liked Eric. Jacob had been a jerk to me and we'd both hurt each other. The last thing I should care about was if Jacob remembered my birthday or not.

I almost knocked over a girl on the sidewalk and I didn't even stop to apologize. I couldn't think about this right now. Had to put it away. But what if . . . no.

"No," I said aloud, not caring if anyone saw me and thought I was crazy for talking to myself.

I.

Did.

Not.

Like.

Jacob.

By the time I got to history class, I considered that hyper-ventilation might be a possibility. I didn't want to go to class with Eric and Jacob. We had assigned seats—Eric was two rows away and three seats in front of me. Jacob was in the next row and one seat behind me. They'd ig-nored each other every class we'd had so far.

When I got into the classroom, a few people were already inside. Jacob was sitting at his desk, flipping through the reading from last night. Eric wasn't here yet.

"Hey," he said.

I ignored him, not turning back to look. But a tiny part of me wanted to.

"Just . . . happy birthday," he said.

My chest fluttered and I took my time picking out a pen. Today was definitely a pink pen day. I was too afraid to look at Jacob. I couldn't give away even the slightest clue that I'd questioned my feelings about him. Finally, I twisted back to look at him. "Thanks," I said, turning back around before he had time to say a word.

More students came into the room, then Eric walked

in. His grin was so wide when he saw me—it made me hate myself for considering that I might like Jacob. Even for one second.

"Happy birthday, Sash!" Eric said. He dropped his bag on his chair and hurried over to give me a hug.

"Thank you! But we're not celebrating yet, remember?" I said, clinging to him for a few seconds longer than usual.

"I know," he said. "I'm sure Paige and Callie are planning the best party ever. And you'll have to wait till then for your present."

"Oooh," I said. "But don't know you know my rule?"

Eric crossed his arms. "Tell me, Sasha Silver. What's your 'rule'?"

"That anytime is present time," I said. "And I'll gladly accept your gift today. It'll take the burden off you from having to, you know, keep it in your room and stuff. Clutter. Bad."

Eric laughed. "That's it. I'm walking away from you now."

"But!" I called after him, laughing. "A hint?"

"We can't talk anymore," Eric said, pretend-*shhh*ing me. "The teacher will be here any second. I'm not serving detention with you on your birthday."

I stuck out my tongue at him.

I took out my phone as the teacher, Mr. Spellman, walked in. I texted under my desk. *Cal wants 2 do a group date nite on Fri. Me. U. Cal. Jacob. Paige. Ryan. U in?*

I watched Eric type back. *Totally worth it just to spend time w u.*

I had the best guy. A girl couldn't ask for a better boyfriend and I was never going to think about Jacob again. I was with the right guy. No doubt.

"I want to start by talking about an upcoming group project," Mr. Spellman said. "In a few weeks, you'll turn in a paper and will present your research to the class. Each person will have a different job, from researching, to writing, to typing, to preparing the PowerPoint you'll need to present to the class."

Mr. Spellman stepped over to his dark cherry wood desk and picked up a folder. "I've broken up the class. You should trade contact info with your partners so that you're ready to start working soon."

I looked over at Eric.

"First group," Mr. Spellman said. "Kaavya, Leesa, Roger, and Wess."

He went through a few more people and with every name that was called that wasn't mine, Jacob's, or Eric's,

I shrank into my chair. There was *no* way we'd all end up in the same group. None.

"Next," Mr. Spellman said. He ran his finger down the page. "Eric, Aaron, Taylor . . ."

Safe so far . . .

"And Jacob."

I almost let my head slam into my desk. That was the WORST possible group! Ever!

I looked at Eric whose eyes were on Jacob's. Both guys glared at each other. I tried not to squirm, but I was stuck between them.

For a second, I thought one of the guys would ask for a new group. I didn't even hear Mr. Spellman call my name or announce my partners. What was going to happen when my sort-of-ex and current boyfriend were forced to work together?

9

DON'T MAKE ME SLAP YOU

LATER THAT AFTERNOON, I UNHOOKED A tacked-up Charm from the crossties. Our lesson was on the outdoor course today. And for once, I felt ready. I loved jumping and so did Charm. Plus, I was still basking in my birthday glow.

I'd finally let myself relax and the afternoon had been perfect. Mom and Dad had called during lunch and they'd both sang the *entire* happy birthday song. They said Paige had e-mailed them about my party and my presents from them would be there. I smiled to myself. Things were finally feeling right again.

My phone buzzed on top of my tack trunk and I grabbed it to check the message before class. It was from Paige.

RYAN SAID YES!!! OMG!!!!

I typed back. *Of course he said Y 2 Paige Parker! Yaaay!*

A quick squeeze of panic gripped my chest, then it disappeared. My happiness for Paige won over my nerves about the night out with Callie and Jacob.

I stuck my phone inside my tack trunk and led Charm out of the stable. It was cooler today and I was glad—the days of intense heat were exhausting on both horse and rider.

Jasmine led Phoenix next to me and I noticed her breeches. They were the warm-up breeches that Callie and I had been drooling over since we'd seen them in an issue of *Young Rider*. They were black, but the insides of the knees were pink and covered with tiny silver stars. We couldn't wear those to shows, but Mr. Conner didn't mind if we wore fun breeches to practice. All of mine were basic—black, brown, white, navy. But Jasmine's new pair was envy-worthy.

"Haven't seen you around the Winchester common room much," Jas said. "Are you sneaking off to spend every free second with your boyfriend?"

"No," I said. "I've been busy with little things like homework and riding."

"So you're *not* hanging out with Eric? Huh." Jas smirked. "Interesting."

"I didn't say that," I said. "I said I wasn't spending *every single second* with him. I'm not clingy like that."

I halted Charm, mounted, and rode him away from Jasmine to warm up. What she'd said made *no* sense. Interesting? How?! *Whatever,* I told myself. *Ignore her.*

Heather showed up seconds later on Aristocrat and the three of us spent ten minutes warming up the horses before Mr. Conner started the lesson.

"Let's work on a few practice jumps," he said. He wore a Canterwood Crest baseball cap to shield his eyes from the sun.

"Heather, you'll ride first. Then, Jasmine and Sasha. Everyone's horses are properly warmed up, correct?"

"Yes," we said.

"Good," Mr. Conner said. "Jas and Sasha, move to the side of the arena. Heather, you can begin when you're ready."

Jasmine and I trotted Phoenix and Charm to the side of the arena and turned them to face the five jumps Mr. Conner had set up. Three verticals of increasing height and two oxers.

Heather circled Aristocrat once before letting him straighten and approach the first fence. His canter was smooth and she collected him well before the jump.

Aristocrat leaped it easily and moved toward the second jump—a taller vertical with yellow and white poles. They took the highest vertical and Heather let his speed increase a fraction to give him enough momentum to get over the oxer. Aristocrat's chestnut mane whipped into the air as the gelding jumped, his knees tucked and his body relaxed on the landing. He asked for more rein before the second oxer, but Heather held him back.

"Nice work," Mr. Conner said. Heather dipped her head in thanks and let Aristocrat slow to a trot, then a walk. "Evaluate yourself. What did you do well and what could you improve on?"

Heather halted Aristocrat beside me and looked at Mr. Conner. "He paid attention over every fence, but he was too eager before the first oxer. He wants to go faster when he doesn't need to and he would have been tired on a longer course."

"I agree," Mr. Conner said. "That's an excellent observation, Heather."

Heather smiled and Jas rolled her eyes.

"Jasmine, go ahead," Mr. Conner said. "Please take your time over the course."

Heather and I shot looks at each other. Mr. Conner still thought Jasmine moved too fast over jumps and he constantly reprimanded her about racing through courses. It had cost her a spot on the advanced team this fall when she'd first tried out.

Jasmine, unlike Heather, didn't give Phoenix a circle to settle. She heeled him forward and pointed him at the first jump. Phoenix cleared each one with ease and I was almost transfixed by the way he tackled each jump. His blue glitter bell boots flashed over each jump and I wished I'd put my favorite pink ones on Charm. But I knew he hated them, so I'd put on his green ones.

Jasmine finished the course, and with a triumphant smile, rode back to Heather and me.

"What did you think?" Mr. Conner asked, tapping his clipboard against his leg.

Jasmine pushed back her helmet. "Phoenix was perfect. He didn't miss a step and we applied everything we learned at YENT camp."

Had she met Mr. Conner? Wrong answer.

Mr. Conner frowned. "So there's no room for you or your horse to improve?"

Jasmine was silent for a second. "No, you're right. Sorry. Phoenix is a little eager between fences."

"And?" Mr. Conner prompted.

"And it was my fault for letting him rush," Jas said.

Mr. Conner nodded and his face was serious. "That's a better answer. Let me say something to *all* of you."

We looked at him.

"If you think because you've made the YENT that you're done learning—you're wrong," Mr. Conner said. His voice was low. "The second someone begins to think she has nothing left to learn as a rider, her career is over. There's *always* something to learn. If you think you know everything about riding, then please resign from the YENT. Mr. Nicholson and I will only work with riders who want to grow."

I knew that speech wasn't directed at me. Unlike Jas, I'd never thought for a second that I had nothing to learn. I was the opposite—I felt like I knew *nothing* compared to them. Sometimes, I wondered if Jas was right—no matter what I did, I'd never be a rider who had a shot at the United States Equestrian Team or the Olympics. But it was my dream. I had to keep reminding myself that Jas was just trying to intimidate me off the team.

Across the arena, I watched someone walk through the grass and stop at the arena fence.

Callie.

She climbed the fence and sat on the top rail. She waved at us, then sat still—watching. There was no rule that said you couldn't observe lessons, but it would have tortured me to watch people ride when I couldn't. And I could barely stand to look at her. She'd be in the arena right now if it weren't for me. But I knew why she was here—Callie was showing up to support me. After I'd told her how alone I'd felt, she'd come to be an ally. Even though she couldn't practice with us, she was doing whatever she could to make me feel better.

"Sasha," Mr. Conner said. "You may go."

I trotted Charm forward, my eyes meeting Callie's. She gave me a thumbs-up and mouthed, *You got it.*

Callie was trying to help, but her presence rattled me. I tried to focus and concentrate on Charm. I let him into a canter and he approached the first vertical. We soared into the air and when we landed, he tugged the reins and increased his speed. We didn't have enough distance between jumps and he took off a half second too late before the second vertical. His knees knocked the plastic rail and it tumbled to the ground with a *thunk*.

I did half halt, easing him, and his long strides propelled us to the next jump. We flashed by Callie and I tried not to look at her. *Focus!* I yelled at myself. I stared between the tips of Charm's ears and looked ahead at the next jump.

I started counting strides. *Three, two, one, now!* I shoved my hands up along Charm's neck and leaned forward, lifting my seat slightly out of the saddle. Charm jumped, landed cleanly, and we cantered to the final oxer.

Charm snorted and asked for more rein. I gave him some and let him build a bit more speed to get over the oxer. He rocked back on his haunches and upward. His body stretched over the oxer's spread and he landed softly on the other side.

"Good boy," I said, patting his neck.

"Nice," Mr. Conner said. "What did you think?"

I rested my hands on Charm's withers. "I lost focus and that's why he knocked the rail. But he didn't let it affect the oxer and he didn't lose his confidence after we pulled down the rail."

"That's true," Mr. Conner said. "But don't be so hard on yourself. You did lose concentration and he took advantage of it, but we need to work with him to keep *his* focus, even if you lose yours for a few seconds."

I nodded. Mr. Conner was obviously trying to make me feel better.

"Let's run through a couple of flat work exercises, then we'll stop for today," Mr. Conner said. "Space out and do a sitting trot."

I sat to Charm's trot and we passed Callie. I tried not to look at her and to keep my focus on Charm. Charm, always in tune to my moods, stiffened and let his trot switch from smooth to bumpy. I took a breath, forcing myself to relax in the saddle, but I couldn't when Callie was watching. Every time we went by her, I felt a surge of guilt.

"Sasha," Mr. Conner called. "Pull Charm to a walk, then ask him for a trot again."

I flushed. It was a beginner mistake. I shouldn't have any problems with a sitting trot by now. I slowed Charm, and Jasmine edged around us, trotting by and cutting in front of us. Phoenix's tail streamed behind him and, unlike Aristocrat, he didn't swish his tail in Charm's face when Jasmine forced him in our path.

I asked Charm to trot, and this time I pushed my tailbone into the saddle and focused on keeping my hands light. I stayed relaxed and forced Callie out of my brain. She was here for support—not to rattle me—and that's how I had to take it.

"Posting trot," Mr. Conner called. "Trot for a lap, then cross over the center and reverse directions."

Heather, Jasmine and I started posting. I found the right lead immediately and rose and fell with Charm's shoulder. Ahead of me, Aristocrat tossed his head and tried to jump into a canter.

Mr. Conner didn't need to tell Heather what to do. She tightened the reins, pulled Aristocrat in a circle, and made him settle before realigning him along the wall. Heather was in total control after that.

Mr. Conner worked us for another half hour before dismissing class. "Good work, everyone, and I'll see you tomorrow."

I rode Charm up to Callie and she smiled at me. "Good practice," she said.

"But we knocked the rail and—"

"Omigod," Callie interrupted, holding up a hand. "Don't make me slap you. You knocked *one* rail. It happens! Stop it."

I grinned. "Thanks. I needed that."

And that's why Callie was my BFF—she knew how to handle my freak-outs.

"Awww, this is just *so* cute," Jas said, riding up beside me. She halted Phoenix, and he and Charm sniffed muzzles. They got along even though Jas and I couldn't stand each other. I liked Phoenix, too. I just thought he needed a different owner.

"What?" I asked.

"Your BFF who didn't even make the YENT showed up to be 'supportive.' But really? Be honest, Callie."

Callie glared at her. "About what, Jas?" she snapped.

"You're here to watch Sasha self-destruct. You're waiting for Mr. Conner to finally kick her off the team so you can take her spot. Just be real about it, Cal. That fake BFF attitude is so obnox."

Callie jumped off the fence and walked up to Phoenix. She held his reins under his chin, stroking his neck.

"Excuse you!" Jas said. "Let go of my horse."

But Callie ignored her and kept petting Phoenix.

"I feel sorry for you, honestly," Callie said. "You have no friends and you don't know what it's like to support someone else. I'm not going to argue with you about what you said because you *truly* don't know better."

Callie let go of Phoenix and I dismounted. Together, we walked Charm out of the arena.

Callie sighed. "You know not to pay attention to that girl, right?" she asked.

"I know," I said. "She's ridic. Whatever. She's just trying to break us up and make me miserable. I worried about her before, but I'm over it."

I could feel Callie nodding behind me. "Good. You can't even waste your time on Jas."

Back at the stable, Callie and I walked Charm up and down the aisle to cool him out. We crosstied him and Callie grabbed his tack box while I stayed with him. We were the best grooming team ever. Whenever Callie wasn't looking, I watched her. She was truly happy even though she wasn't on the YENT and one mistake—one mix-up with a lie would ruin that. The on-and-off anxiety I felt about keeping the secrets was worth it. Otherwise, we'd never have moments like these again.

"Want to go to the Sweet Shoppe?" she asked. "I think we need a treat after this crazy week."

"Definitely," I said. "If you want to put Charm in his stall, I'll go drop off his tack."

Callie unclipped Charm and I gathered his saddle, bridle, and pad into my arms. I put away his tack, vowing to clean it tomorrow. My phone buzzed and I opened it to see a text.

From Jacob.

Sry I freaked u out @ lunch b4. Txt me back so I know ur not mad?

I deleted the message without replying and turned off my phone. I tried to take calming breaths. Part of me wanted to text him back because I didn't want him to think I was mad, but I couldn't keep responding to him.

Callie met me in the aisle. "You okay?"

"Totally," I lied. "I just remembered that I have a quiz in English tomorrow and I have to study when we're done."

"What's it on?" Callie asked. "Maybe I already read the book."

"Uh . . ." I was the worst liar ever! "Um, it's on *The Secret Garden*."

At least we were actually reading that book in class.

Callie shook her head. "Sorry. Haven't read it. But you'll do fine. And no stressing about it while we eat."

"Deal." We linked arms and walked down the sidewalk. For the next hour, I wasn't going to worry. I was ready to have fun with my BFF.

10

ENTER JACOB,
STAGE RIGHT

BY THE TIME I SLID INTO MY SEAT FOR MY FIRST
health class on Friday, I was exhausted. I *never* thought I'd
say it, but I actually wished I could go home for the weekend just to get away from everything.

Paige and I walked into the class together and sat
beside each other.

"This is going to be *interesting*," Paige said. "Because . . .
you know."

"Because of our teacher?"

Julia walked into the classroom, looking for an
empty desk. She sat a couple of seats away from Paige
and me.

"*Any* class with Ms.—"

But I didn't finish my sentence. Jacob had just walked

into the classroom. He saw Paige and me and walked over, taking a desk in the next aisle, next to me.

Of course.

Ms. Utz walked into the room with a massive stack of papers in her hands. She tossed them onto her desk with a thump and gave us a crooked smile, baring giant square teeth. She'd paired black dress pants with a collared white shirt—fine so far—and then . . . she'd gone for the purple Crocs. I shuddered.

"Welcome to your weekly health class," Ms. Utz said. "We're going to have fun learning about the human body, nutrition, and exercise."

Paige and I traded grins and then looked back at Utz. She was way too excited about this.

"You'll also learn CPR and basic first aid. Wouldn't want your best friend to croak if you could help it, right?"

Everyone's eyes widened collectively.

"Let's get started," Ms. Utz said. "Read the first chapter to yourselves. In twenty minutes, we'll do an exercise. While you read, I'll be readying the CPR dummy for the class after yours."

I opened my book. We read to ourselves, but really spent most of the time watching Utz try to assemble a scary-looking CPR dummy. I was *not* putting my mouth on that thing—no way!

About twenty minutes later, Utz had finished assembling the dummy.

"The first thing we're going to do is learn how to take someone's pulse," Utz said. "Turn to the person to your right. That's your partner for today's exercise. Introduce yourselves."

With a sigh, I turned to Jacob.

He grinned. "Hi," he said, sticking out his hand. "I'm Jacob Schwartz. And you are?"

"Stop it," I said. I reached to grab a pen from the top of my desk, but Jacob grabbed my hand. His warm fingers enveloped mine until I jerked my hand out of his grasp.

"Everyone, take your partner's hand," Ms. Utz said.

Jacob shot a triumphant look in my direction.

I shot him a look and gave him my hand.

"Place your second and third finger on your partner's wrist, right below the thumb. Press lightly and you should feel a pulse. When you've found your partner's pulse, then let the other person find yours."

Jacob turned my hand over and brushed two fingers down my palm to my wrist. I took a deep breath, but couldn't stop goose bumps from appearing on my arms.

He pressed his fingers lightly against my wrist and looked at me. "Your heart's beating fast," he said.

I pulled my hand back. "No, it's not. Let me do yours so we can be done."

Jacob offered me his arm and I pressed my fingers against his skin. Nothing. I moved my fingers around, pausing in several different places, but I couldn't find his pulse.

"I think you're dead," I said. "'Cause I can't find anything." I raised my hand.

"Yes, Sasha?" Ms. Utz asked.

"I can't find Jacob's pulse."

"Okay, this might occur for some of you," Ms. Utz said. "If you can't locate a person's pulse on his or her wrist, then you'll need to check the carotid artery at the neck."

"Put two fingers below the ear, right below the jaw," Ms. Utz said. "Go ahead, Sasha."

The whole class turned to watch me and I felt my face begin to burn.

I leaned forward and swallowed, putting two fingers on Jacob's neck. His skin was warm under my fingertips. Immediately, I felt a pulse.

"Found it," I said, pulling my fingers away and sliding back—waaay back—into my chair.

Paige looked over at me. *You okay?* she mouthed.

"Totally," I whispered.

Ms. Utz helped the rest of the students find one another's pulses and I paged through my syllabus. If there was even the slightest hint that we had to learn mouth-to-mouth on someone other than Dummy Dan, I was going to find a way out of this class.

Later in the day, I made my way to the theater building. This was just a brief informational meeting about the drama elective, then the class would be held on Mondays and Fridays. I'd been looking forward to the meeting all week. No one I knew was going to be in it—none of my friends were into drama. I'd finally have a class to myself.

As I walked up to the theater building, I couldn't help but stare. It was one of the most gorgeous buildings on campus. Long steps with intricate black iron rails led up to two red doors. Above the doors, there was a peak that stretched to the sky.

I felt a tiny shudder of nerves as I pulled open the door. Sure, I'd watched a zillion movies and had taken a film class, but that might not translate to anything on stage. I could be the worst actress ever. Like, Razzie Award bad. I rolled my eyes at myself. This was going to be fun. I needed to stop being a dork and worrying about everything.

I tugged open the heavy door and stepped inside, noticing how chilly it was in the enormous building. I walked past the closed ticket counter and entered the auditorium. A long staircase of carpeted red stairs with a gleaming dark wooden handrail led toward the stage. A group of students were already clustered near the front of the stage, so I walked down the aisle and sat behind some of them.

I glanced around and my gaze froze on the back of a familiar blond head.

"You're taking this class?" I asked.

Heather turned around, her dangly earrings swirling. "Deal with it, Silver."

"But," I said. "Do you even *like* theater?"

Heather glared. "Omigod, why do you care?"

"Forget it," I said.

I picked up the handbooks that had been required for the class—*The Guide for Young Actors* and *A History of Theater*. I paged through them.

"Hey, Sash."

The voice almost made me drop the books. *Not again.*

Jacob dropped his fave messenger bag—the one

covered in Japanese art—on the floor and took the seat next to me.

"What are you doing here?" I asked.

Jacob tugged down the hem of his black T-shirt. "This sounded like a cool class."

"Theater? But . . ." I lowered my voice so no one else would overhear. "Won't going on stage make you nervous?"

"We won't be acting the whole time. We'll be learning about theater—all of it. Even the behind-the-scenes stuff."

"Yeah, I guess so."

I sat back, trying to pretend that Jacob wasn't next to me. But *Jacob* in theater?! Seriously. I'd picked this class on purpose because I didn't expect anyone I knew—*least* of all Jacob or Heather—to be here.

I looked away from Jacob when a woman walked onto the stage, stopping in the center. Her dark brown hair was superstraight—I wondered if I could get a flatiron rec—and it touched down just to her collarbone. She wore giant silver hoop earrings and her red lipstick made her pale skin look Snow White gorgeous. She looked young enough to be in college.

"Hey, guys!" she said. She smiled at us and waved. "I'm your drama teacher, Ms. Scott. Welcome to my class."

She walked toward the edge of the stage.

"This is *not* a class for you if you intend to coast," Ms. Scott said. "It's a class that revolves around participation in theater games, reading assignments, and group projects."

Everyone nodded. I knew before I'd signed up for her class that drama would be lots of work. But I didn't care. I was kind of looking forward to the distraction.

Ms. Scott waved her hand at us. "C'mon. Everyone get up on stage. We're going to play an improv icebreaker game."

I got up, stepping over Jacob before he could move. A group of about fifteen of us gathered on stage. The dark wooden floor was polished to a deep sheen and thick red velvet curtains hung behind us. The lights were dimmed enough so that we could see the rows and rows of seats that stretched across the theater, all the way up to the balcony section.

Heather stood across from me and Jacob stood a couple of people away from her. I attempted to ignore both of them, sticking my hands in the back pockets of my jeans.

Ms. Scott clapped her hands once and looked at us. "Okay, we'll play games almost every class. The games are supposed to be fun, so don't be nervous."

Jacob's hands were jammed in his pockets and he looked like he wanted to throw up.

"We'll use this icebreaker to build trust and get to know one another's names," Ms. Scott continued. "We're going to use our names and alliteration. So, for example, if I were to introduce myself to you with my first name, I'd say 'Hi, I'm Cool Courtney.'"

We all smiled.

"So, you repeat the person's name before you and then say your own, okay?"

"Okay," we said.

"All right. Let's go. I'll reintroduce myself as your teacher. I'm Social Ms. Scott." She turned to a girl next to her. "Your turn."

The girl grinned. "She's Social Ms. Scott and I'm Writer Whitney."

My turn. "She's Writer Whitney and I'm Sassy Sasha."

We kept going around the circle and then it came to Heather. "He's Awesome Aidan and I'm Hot Heather."

I snorted.

When it came to Jacob, his face was red. He'd made the biggest mistake signing up for this class. Maybe he was trying to get over being shy, but theater class was a huge leap. He could have taken a beginner speech course or something. But I felt for him the second he started blushing.

"She's Lovely Lexa and I'm . . ." his eyes met mine and I wanted to help him, to shout something so he wouldn't be standing there with us staring at him.

"I'm Jammin' Jacob," he said, spitting it out.

The class smiled at his answer and we moved on to the next person. The relief on his face was obvious.

Ms. Scott made the game fun and each person's answer was silly—it definitely *did* break the ice and by the end, I remembered almost everyone's name.

"Okay," Ms. Scott said when everyone had said his or her name. "It's Friday and it's been a long week for all of you, I'm sure. You may go, but please check your syllabus for the reading assignment and be prepared for Monday."

I walked off stage, hurried down the stairs, and left the theater before Jammin' Jacob could corner me again.

11

WHAT QUIZ?

"I HATE ALL OF MY CLOTHES AND I LOOK HORRIBLE in everything!" Paige wailed.

I got up and walked over to her, putting my hands on her shoulders and staring into her eyes.

"You. Do. Not. C'mon, look." I picked a short black shirt and clover green tank top off her bed. The tank top had lacy straps and the green made Paige's red hair look gorgeous. I waved the outfit in front of her. "Wear it."

"Really?" Paige took the clothes from me and slid into them. "You like it?"

I nodded as she checked out her reflection in the mirror. "You look gorgeous. It's perfect for a group night out. Not too dressy or too casual."

I pulled on my own date clothes—a black capped-sleeve shirt, a ruffled black skirt, and pink peep-toe ballet flats.

"I'm *so* nervous!" Paige said. She stood in front of our closet mirror and applied a peachy coat of lip gloss.

"Don't be," I said. "I'll be there and so will Callie. It's just a group thing. Not even a date. We're all just . . . hanging out."

"Hanging out." Paige repeated my words, then smiled at me. "Thanks."

"Anytime."

I'd been hiding my own nerves all night. I didn't want to blow this for Paige. It was her first shot at a chance with Ryan and I wasn't going to let my worries about being around Jacob affect our night.

But no matter how tonight played out, *I* knew I was hiding Jacob's e-mails and texts from Callie, and even Paige. I couldn't help but feel the guilt growing in my stomach. Plus, if the guys were weird to each other, the night would go on *forever*.

It was twilight when Paige and I made our way across campus. Lightning bugs sparkled through the air and lit up the lawn.

"You'll be great," I told Paige. "Don't be nervous. Ryan already really likes you—it's so obvious."

"Really?" Paige tucked her hair behind her ear. "I hope so. I just want to have fun."

"We will."

And I actually started to believe it myself. I'd barely seen Eric since school had begun and my excitement about seeing him was beginning to ease my tension about the night.

When Paige and I walked up to the front of The Slice, Callie was already waiting outside. She looked perfect as always these days: black patent leather ankle boots, black tights, a purple mini, and a black ruffle top.

"Hey," she said, hugging us. "The boys obviously ditched us."

We laughed. "Totally," Paige said. "They went out for a guys' night instead."

"As long as we have pizza and soda, I think I'll survive," Callie said. "School was a *killer* this week."

Paige nodded her head in agreement. "This was the most intense 'welcome back' week ever. The work was crazy even for Canterwood."

"Ohhh, how was your English quiz?" Callie asked. "I forgot to ask Sasha how it went. She said she was nervous about that yesterday. It's crazy that you guys had a quiz the first week."

Omigod.

Paige looked over at me. "What English quiz? We didn't have a quiz today."

I played with a lock of my hair, trying not to panic. "Ugh, I was so tired. I got the dates mixed up. I totally thought we had a quiz on *The Secret Garden* today and I told Callie that we did."

Callie laughed. "I get it. I almost went to English instead of math because I got my schedule confused yesterday."

We giggled and I ran my fingers through my hair, hoping they wouldn't see how much I was sweating. I knew Paige and Callie didn't suspect that I was lying—they honestly believed I'd made a mistake. And while I was glad they didn't guess that I was lying to them, I realized they believed me because they trusted me, which made me feel awful.

"Hi," Jacob said, walking up to us. Callie slipped her fingers through his.

I took a tiny step away from Callie and Jacob, moving closer to Paige. I did not want to do the weird small-talk thing. Jacob and I had nothing to say to each other and I didn't want to talk to him at *all* in front of Callie. But I didn't have to wait long—Eric and Ryan showed up right as I was getting ready to text Eric.

"Hey!" I said to both of them a little too enthusiastically.

Eric smiled at everyone—even at Jacob.

"Hi," Ryan said. His eyes went right to Paige. He stepped in front of her and pulled open the door, motioning her to step inside first.

We all walked into The Slice, waited for a hostess and then followed her to a round table near the back. Eric was next to me, then Callie, Jacob, Paige, and Ryan.

The smells of pizza, buffalo wings, and mozzarella sticks were mouthwatering. Plus, the place was adorable—all of the tablecloths had red and white checkers on them. In the center of our table, an old-fashioned lantern gave off a soft glow. The restaurant was quiet and didn't have the same level of sugar-high chatter that the Sweet Shoppe had. It was low-key—just the kind of atmosphere I wanted for tonight.

"I love it here," I said.

"Me too," Ryan said.

We asked for sodas and told the waiter we needed a couple of minutes to decide what to order.

"How about we get three different pizzas to share," Ryan suggested. "That way we all get a ton of options."

"Yes! I love that idea, Ryan!" Paige blurted out. Even

the low lighting couldn't hide the pinkness that spread over her face.

"Me too," I said, jumping in. "Cool with you guys?" I looked at Eric, Jacob, and Callie.

"Let's do it," Callie said.

Eric slid a menu into the middle of the table and we all leaned forward to decide.

Under the table, I felt Eric reach for my hand. He squeezed it and I looked over at him. When our eyes met, I wanted to kiss him. In front of everyone—I didn't even care. But guilt about hiding Jacob's messages settled immediately into my stomach. Suddenly, I wasn't so hungry anymore.

"You know what we want, right?" Eric asked.

"Absolutely," I said, forcing a smile.

"Sasha and I are going to get pepperoni and extra cheese," he said.

Callie, Ryan, and Paige nodded.

Jacob laughed. "Extra cheese," he muttered. "Perfect."

"What does *that* mean?" Eric asked. He let go of my hand, his shoulders tensing.

"Nothing, man. Whatever." Jacob shook his head, smiling to himself.

Callie looked at him, her face showing her embarrassment. Our eyes met.

Sorry, she mouthed.

I shook my head. *It's fine,* I mouthed back.

"Um," Callie started. "Jacob and I are ordering Hawaiian."

Jacob, Callie, and I looked over at Paige and Ryan. Their heads were bent together and they were talking in tones low enough that I couldn't hear them.

"What are you guys getting?" I asked Paige.

She looked up as if she was confused that someone was talking to her. "What? Sorry."

I smiled. "I just asked what you guys want to order."

"Oops," Ryan said. "We didn't even decide yet." He turned to Paige. "What would you like? I'll eat any kind of pizza."

"Veggie okay?" Paige asked.

"Veggie it is," Ryan said.

The waiter came over and pulled a notepad from his apron. "What can I get for you?"

We all looked at one another, deciding who was going to order. Everyone's eyes just seemed to settle on Eric.

"Okay," Eric said. "We'll have the—"

"I guess someone appointed himself the one in charge," Jacob interrupted.

Omigod. Why was Jacob being such a jerk?!

"Jacob," I snapped. "What's your deal?"

I closed my mouth, surprised that I'd just called him out like that. Callie glanced at me and shot me another *I'm sorry* look. She turned and glared at Jacob.

Eric sat back in his chair, arms folded. "Jacob, this is obviously important to you, so go ahead. Please."

I'd *known* this group date idea was bad. But I'd really thought the guys would be able to at least fake coolness with each other. This was ridic! Paige and Ryan, looking up, finally seemed to catch on to the tension. They fell silent, which was the last thing I wanted for Paige's first date. This night was supposed to be about getting Paige and Ryan together and for us to have fun as friends.

Jacob stared at Eric for what felt like hours before looking at the waiter. He placed our orders and the table was quiet.

"So," Callie said, her tone too cheery, "Sasha and I were saying the other day how we've had zero time to hang out with friends this week. I was delusional thinking that Canterwood teachers wouldn't drown us with homework on the first week."

That made everyone laugh. Phew—something everyone could agree on.

"I know," I said. "Paige is my roommate and we

barely got to see each other this week. That's def got to change."

Jacob sipped Coke from his plastic red glass and set it down. "I actually got to see Callie a lot this week, but I haven't seen much of my other friends." He looked at me. "Besides Sasha. We saw each other at lunch on Tuesday."

I nodded once, then I looked over at Ryan. "How's your first week back?" I asked Ryan.

He smiled. "The same as every year. Completely insane until I get used to my schedule. But I think it'll be calmer next week." His eyes shifted over to Paige for a second. "I'll have more time to go out."

Paige smiled and I forced myself not to cheer. Ryan *sooo* like-liked her. I gave them five seconds alone before he asked her out. Perfect! Across the table, Callie had picked up on Ryan's comment too. She winked at me.

Beside me, Eric frowned. He shifted in his seat and looked at me. "Jacob said he saw you at lunch on Tuesday?"

I nodded. "Yeah. For, like, five seconds."

I had no idea where Eric was going with this. He *couldn't* be jealous that I'd seen Jacob at lunch. If only he knew how much I'd been avoiding that scenario. I'd done nothing wrong—I'd told Jacob to leave and he had.

Eric turned in his seat, staring at me. "Callie and I had to have a later lunch on Tuesday because of science class. Didn't you text me that you skipped lunch that day?"

Did I?

I felt the burning panic in my chest. I'd lied and had forgotten about it. I *had* told him that I'd skipped lunch. That was the most unnecessary thing to lie about, but I'd done it to avoid telling Eric that Jacob and I had been alone together for even five minutes.

I turned to Eric, my mouth hanging open. I couldn't come up with a lie fast enough! "I—"

"I'm an idiot," Jacob interjected. "It wasn't lunch." He paused, thinking. "I saw you at the vending machine and I joked about how *that* was your lunch."

Our eyes met for a brief second, then I looked down at the table.

Ten minutes ago, I'd been a jerk to Jacob and he'd just saved me. He knew I'd lied and he covered for me anyway.

"Right," I said. "I got a gross package of stale cheese crackers."

Eric's gaze shifted back and forth between Jacob and me. "But two minutes ago you didn't deny seeing Jacob at lunch."

I felt like we were one of those couples fighting in front of friends and making everyone else uncomfortable.

"It didn't seem important to say 'Hey, I saw you at the vending machine and not the caf.'" I shrugged and sipped my drink.

Eric looked at me for another second as if he wanted to say something else, but the waiter appeared at that moment with our pizzas. We all took a slice of each and started eating. Callie, Eric, Jacob, and I kept our eyes mostly on our food while Paige and Ryan continued their bubbly conversation. I didn't want to ruin the night for Paige and have her feel sorry for me—someone else had to start talking too.

"The weather's been awful lately," I said. Lamest. Topic. Ever. "I'm always a mess after lessons."

"Yeah, at least I get one coolish lesson in the morning," Callie said. "Afternoon lessons are beyond gross."

Callie and I looked at the guys, waiting for them to at least say *something*. But they stared at their glasses and Eric swirled his straw in his Coke.

It was Friday night.

And we were talking about the weather.

12

SPARKLE FREE

split the bill and left The Slice. We walked outside and stood in a ragged circle outside the restaurant. I was glad it was dark outside—it helped hide whatever lingering stress was showing on my face from dinner.

"So, Jacob and I are going to catch a movie," Callie said. "Tonight was so much fun!" I knew my BFF well enough to realize when she was being fake-cheery.

"Yeah!" I chimed in. My own excitement was as real as hers. "So much fun." I glanced at Paige and Ryan. "Eric, want to walk to the courtyard with me?"

"Sure," Eric said, taking my hand. I waved at Callie as she as Jacob walked off toward the media center.

Ryan turned immediately to Paige. "Can I walk you back to your dorm?"

Paige's wide eyes darted to me. I nodded slightly and raised my eyebrows.

"Sure," Paige said. "That would be great."

Ryan and Paige started down the sidewalk and Paige looked back over her shoulder at me. I smiled and waved her on.

Seeing Paige so happy made the entire uncomfortable evening worth it.

"Paige is hilarious," Eric said. "She's a TV star and a great girl who has always given you good advice, but she couldn't be more freaked out about being around a guy."

"I know. But she'll relax once she gets to know Ryan. She does give great advice, but it's different when it's *you*."

Still holding hands, Eric and I walked down the streetlight-lit sidewalk. The campus was quiet tonight; only a few students were walking around.

"I'm glad we have time to go out just by ourselves," I said. "I missed you this week."

"Me too," Eric said. "Things *will* settle down, though. And hey, sorry about the weirdness over the lunch thing. I wasn't trying to make a big deal out of it, but I know it came out that way."

I hated that he was the one apologizing right now. I

should have been the one telling *him* the truth. "It's cool," I said. "Forget about it."

As we walked together, I loved how good it felt to be with him. Maybe I had been confused for a minute or two—thinking I might still have feelings for Jacob. But it had only been because Jacob had been the first guy I'd ever liked. There was history between us and now the *only* thing I felt for Jacob was friendship.

"How are you feeling now about the YENT?" Eric asked. "I could tell you were tense this week."

I slowed a little. "I'm feeling better. At first, I couldn't stop being intimidated by Heather and Jas. It messed up Charm and we fell apart."

"But you know you've got nothing to worry about. You were chosen for the YENT, Sash. Mr. Conner and Mr. Nicholson both know how good you are."

We stopped by a bench and sat down. I snuggled against Eric's shoulder—he rubbed my upper arm.

"How are your classes?" I asked Eric.

"They're all pretty good so far," he said. "I like science a lot. Callie and I sit next to each other and text whenever the teacher does something dumb."

"Oh," I said, trying to laugh. But it made me nervous that they were texting! "Like what?"

Eric grinned. "A couple of days ago, he was supposed to pass out a study sheet for a quiz we're going to have next week."

I nodded.

"Except he accidentally handed out one answer sheet to the quiz and everyone started passing it around."

"Omigod! Did he get it back?"

"Yeah, some girl got it and turned it in. He canceled the quiz, obviously."

"Score for you, then."

Eric rubbed his hand over the back of my head. "What about you? Things okay with classes with the YENT schedule and everything?"

"So far. I mean, we haven't started prepping for a show yet, so I don't know how that's going to be. But I'll deal with it when we get there. Our first show is going to be a schooling show, so that'll be a nice transition into competition season."

"Definitely. And Mr. Conner said he'd give the advanced team our first show date soon. I'd love to practice with you on the weekends, if that's cool."

I smiled. "You better."

"Let's get you back to your dorm before you're too tired to practice at all," Eric said.

I sighed. "Ugh—but true; if I don't get my beauty rest I'll do so poorly at practice Mr. Conner will kick me out for good."

Eric laughed and reached out a hand to pull me up. "Totally. And then I'd never see you again, which would be devastating."

I mock-rolled my eyes. "Uh-huh. I'm sure."

We walked back to Winchester and I started up the stairs, but Eric grabbed my hand, pulling me back gently and turning me toward him.

He leaned into me and our lips touched. I waited for the overwhelming feeling of sparkles and the tiny shock waves that I always felt when Eric's lips were against mine. But I felt . . . nothing. I pulled back, trying not to show the disappointment on my face.

"'Night," Eric said, smiling. "Text you tomorrow."

Wait a sec. He didn't feel that?! He couldn't have missed how off that kiss was. Unless . . . it was just me. OMG. I was so freaked out about my lies that I couldn't even enjoy kissing my own boyfriend anymore.

"Bye."

I stood outside long after he'd walked away, trying to figure out what had just happened. And what it meant for us.

13

BASICALLY, I HAVEN'T BEEN NAUSEOUS FOR A WEEK

ON SATURDAY, THE ONLY THING I WANTED TO do was trail ride with Charm and get away from everyone. I didn't feel like working in the arena, but Mr. Conner would never let me go by myself.

"You sure you're okay?" Paige asked. "We could go to the movies or watch a DVD. You could ride later."

"Can we do that after?" I asked. "That sounds great, but I need to work Charm for a while."

Paige nodded. "Okay. Later for sure."

I left Winchester and walked to the stable. Inside the tack room, I gathered Charm's tack. We'd just have to work in the arena. The door pushed open and Heather walked inside. I wondered . . . no way. She'd *never* say yes to trail riding with me. And did I even want to go with Heather Fox?

Yes.

I was desperate.

"I want to trail ride," I said. "But no one else can go. Want to come with me?"

Heather glanced up from the stirrup leather she was adjusting on Aristocrat's saddle. She stared at me for a second. "Sure. But only because Jasmine took over the arena and I don't want to see her face."

I nodded. "Ditto. Leave in twenty?"

"Fifteen," Heather said. "You're not eighty, Grandma."

"Make it ten."

I groomed Charm and tacked him up. Exactly ten minutes later, I met Heather outside the stable. We mounted our horses and started for the woods. It was barely ten and there was still a slight coolness in the air. We let the horses amble at an easy walk—I wasn't in any hurry to get back to campus.

As we entered the woods and the sounds of campus disappeared, I felt my tension slip away. I could finally breathe. Heather didn't know anything that was going on and she was pretty much the only person I hadn't lied to. This had to be one of the weirdest moments I'd had at Canterwood. Ever.

"So, what's wrong with you, Silver?" Heather asked.

Okay, so I'd been able to relax for about five seconds.

"What? Nothing's wrong."

Heather peered at me from under the brim of her helmet. "You're the worst liar. Really. Or I'm just way smarter than you." She smirked. "Both are true, actually."

The trail started to wind through the woods and we were about to reach the open meadow that was flat and perfect for galloping.

"You're delusional," I said lightly. "Want to race at the field?"

Heather edged Aristocrat closer to Charm. "How many times do we have to play this game? I *know* something's up and you deny it. Eventually, you crack and fess up. I'm *always* right. So just spill already and quit wasting my time."

I didn't know if I wanted to push her off Aristocrat or tell her everything just because I needed someone— anyone—to talk to.

"Guess what? You *can* be wrong. And this time you are."

But she was right. Like always.

The horses walked a few more strides down the dirt trail before Heather sighed. "Okay, fine. *I'll* tell you what's going on."

My fingers tightened around Charm's reins. "Go for it."

Heather looked over, her blue eyes settling on me. "You haven't been making googly eyes at Eric all week, or smiling for no reason, *and* you're not giggling on the phone every five seconds. So, basically, I haven't been nauseous for a week."

I forced myself not to show even the slightest reaction. I knew Heather pretty well by now. But she still surprised me sometimes with her accuracy. Like, scary accurate.

"Maybe I haven't had time to be 'googly-eyed,'" I said. "School just started on Monday and you know how crazy things are. No one has time for anything."

Heather loosened the reins and let Aristocrat stretch his neck. "You haven't seen your boyfriend all summer. Why aren't you following him around everywhere?"

"I never followed him around. And things are *perfect* between Eric and me. We iChatted all summer, text a lot, and we're really happy."

Charm snorted and I leaned down to rub his neck. It was still cool since we were under the shade of the trees.

Heather slowed Aristocrat and turned to me. "Yeah. And you'd be even happier if you weren't into Jacob."

Heather's words, even at a normal tone, seemed to echo

through the woods as if she'd yelled them. Something twisted in my stomach. She was wrong.

"Jacob's with Callie," I said, my voice quiet. "I'm dating Eric and I like him. I'd never go after my best friend's boyfriend."

"Unlike Callie," she spat.

My stomach did a somersault, remembering the moment I'd found out Callie and Jacob were together. But that was history. Ancient history.

Heather looked at me, her gaze softening. "I didn't ask you if you'd try to get Jacob back. I said you liked him. You didn't deny that."

I stared at her. My mouth opened and for seconds, nothing came out.

"I do not like Jacob in that way," I said. "If I ever did, I'd be a horrible friend. And Eric is amazing. He's the perfect guy for me. Jacob and I wouldn't have worked out."

"How do you know?" Heather asked. "If some . . . things hadn't happened, you might still be together."

I paused. I'd never considered that scenario. Not once. Jacob and me—still together. No Eric. I couldn't even imagine what that would be like.

"I guess I don't know," I said, my voice almost a whisper. "But it doesn't matter."

Heather nodded and we let the horses trot down the path. Their hooves were muffled against the dirt trail and we twisted and turned through the woods.

We reached the meadow and drew the horses to a halt. Charm and Aristocrat eyed each other—both horses knew what the field meant.

"Fine, let's race," Heather said. "But you have to admit one thing first." She grinned.

I made a face. "What?"

"You totally don't like Jacob—whatever. But the boy is hot. Say it." Heather dropped Aristocrat's knotted reins on his neck and folded her arms, waiting for my answer.

I rolled my head from side to side, stretching the tension from my neck.

"Fine," I said, finally. "I agree. Happy?"

There. At least I hadn't said directly that Jacob was hot.

And with that, I heeled Charm forward and shoved my hands along his neck. Charm leaped into a gallop, darting away from Heather and Aristocrat.

"Silver!" Heather yelled. "You're dead!" Hoofbeats thundered behind Charm and me and I lowered myself over his neck, giving him all the rein he wanted. Aristocrat and Heather never had a chance to catch us.

14

MAKE A DECISION, ALREADY!

WHEN I GOT BACK TO MY ROOM, PAIGE WAS sprawled on her stomach with her laptop in front of her on her bed.

"Whatcha doing?" I asked. I wondered if maybe now was the time to tell her everything. She'd know how to fix this. And I knew Paige—she could handle listening to me and not project my fears onto her relationship with Ryan.

She grinned. "IMing with Ryan."

My plan to tell her evaporated. Again. I had to stop going back and forth—I was being ridiculous. I needed to stick with my decision. I was *not* going to do that to Paige when she was just getting into her own relationship. Paige had been all about school, volunteering, and hobbies—never about being boy-crazy. She'd liked a boy before she'd come to Canterwood, but she'd gone away to school before she'd had a chance to see if anything would happen. Ryan was her first shot at a real boyfriend.

"Oooh," I said in a teasing voice. "I'll leave you two alone."

Paige rolled her eyes. "Oh, please. Don't go. You just got here. I'll totally be done in a few minutes and we could go see a movie."

"That's cool," I said. "I'm just going to go to the common room for, like, half an hour to catch up on a reading assignment. Come get me when you're done."

Paige looked up from her computer screen. "'Kay."

I grabbed *The Secret Garden* and swiped a notebook. I had to take notes for Mr. Davidson's class. It made me feel less nervous if I went into the class discussion with a few notes on what I wanted to say.

When I got to the common room, I curled up in the window seat and opened my notebook. The lies swirled in my head and I tried to force them out of my brain. I really should have been reading, but I couldn't focus.

"Oooh, writing in your diary?"

I looked up at Jasmine as she walked into the room. Her eyes were on my journal. "Journaling about *The Secret*

Garden for English," I said. "Want to read my deepest, darkest thoughts about Colin and Mary?"

Jas snorted. "I'll pass, thanks." She grabbed a Sprite from the fridge and left.

My gaze went back to the window and I don't know how long I stared outside before Paige came inside. At least fall break wasn't too far away. I'd be able to escape from everything and have fun with Paige in New York—it was exactly what I needed.

"Get a lot done?" she asked.

I stood, nodding. "A lot. Let me grab my purse and we can go."

Paige followed me back to our room. "How was your ride? What'd you do?" she asked.

"Trail ride," I said. "I should have practiced, but I didn't feel like it." I picked up my purse and put it over my shoulder.

"You deserve to trail ride," Paige said. "You love it and so does Charm. You guys practice all week—a break is okay."

"Yeah," I said. "But guess who I went with."

Paige slowed as we left our room and walked down the Winchester hallway. "Callie?"

"Nope."

"Eric?"

"Wrong." I laughed. "Keep going."

"Not . . ." Paige paused, looking at me sideways. "Not Heather or Jasmine."

I nodded. "Heather."

Paige grabbed my arm. "No way! Wow, you must have been totally desperate. She's"—Paige swallowed—"still alive, right?"

I laughed. "Yes! She's fine. It wasn't bad. We didn't talk, really. Just rode out to the field and raced."

Paige looked at me. "You won, didn't you? I can tell."

"I totally won."

15

COURTYARD
GHOSTS

I WAS AWAKE WHEN THE SUN CAME UP THE next morning. I'd tossed and turned for a long time the night before and had finally dozed off. But before I'd fallen asleep, I'd managed to remind myself that every lie I told was in everyone's best interest. And they weren't lies, really . . . just little white lies. Harmless.

I crawled out of bed, got dressed, and grabbed my backpack. I scrawled a note for Paige telling her that I was going to the library and if she wanted to come, she should text me.

Paige didn't even roll over when I tiptoed out the door and shut it softly behind me. The benefit of not being able to sleep—I was awake early and could get my homework out of the way.

I took the long way across campus and passed the

courtyard. Clear water flowed over the stone fountain and made soothing sounds. I saw flashes of orange, white, red, and black as the koi darted around in the small pond near the edge of the courtyard. As I walked, I flashed back to scenes from the last day of school—Eric kissing me good-bye for the summer. The way he smiled when he promised to keep in touch with me. Then, Jacob. Apologizing, asking me for another chance.

I looked away and focused on the sidewalk. There were too many ghosts in the courtyard.

Deciding to be lazy, I took the elevator up to the top floor of the library—the quietest floor where no one wanted to go because it was where the most of the antique books were and it smelled kind of musty.

That's exactly why I wanted to go—no one else would be around.

I walked through the rows of books and ran my fingers along some of the spines. Whispers came from the other side of the shelf and I stopped, trying to keep my shoes from squeaking on the floor.

"... such a ... and it was embarrassing."

It was Jasmine. I almost stopped breathing as I tried to hear what she was saying.

"She should have known . . . and she still came back to Canterwood after YENT camp," Jas continued. "If only you'd seen . . . messed up. I don't even have to . . . Sasha will get herself kicked off the YENT."

I gritted my teeth, trying not to cry. But tears blurred my vision—Jasmine couldn't have hurt my feelings more if she'd tried. I was still sensitive about YENT camp. I felt tears roll down my cheeks and, turning on my heel, I walked down the aisle before Jasmine and whomever she was talking to—probably the Belles—heard me.

I hurtled down the stairs and slammed open the door to the second floor stairwell. I almost smacked straight into someone, but I was too upset to even bother looking up or apologizing. I kept walking toward the stairs.

"Sasha. What's wrong?" Jacob grabbed my upper arm, stopping me from going out the door. His green eyes were locked on my face. I'd never seen him look so concerned.

"Jacob."

At that moment I didn't care if we were "supposed" to be talking, if it was wrong for me to be here with him, or if I was sending mixed signals by pushing him away one minute and talking to him now. I leaned against him, crying.

He lowered me gently to the bottom of the stairs and let me cry against his shoulder, rubbing my upper back. I sobbed until I started to hiccup, then sat up and swiped my hand across my eyes.

"I'm so sorry," I whispered. "I shouldn't have done that. I keep—"

"Sasha," Jacob said. "That's the last thing I care about right now. Tell me what happened."

I clutched my hands in my lap. "I just overheard Jasmine talking about how badly I messed up at YENT camp."

Jacob shook his head. "I'm sure if you messed up at all—she was just exaggerating to make herself feel better."

"No, she was right. It was awful. We were jumping one morning and I got so intimidated by the other riders that I couldn't concentrate. Charm got confused and knocked three rails in a row."

"I'm sorry," Jacob whispered. "That's tough."

My phone vibrated and I pulled it out to check the caller ID. *Paige.*

"It's Paige," I said. "I'll call her back in a sec."

I looked up from my phone to Jacob. Here he was, sitting here and listening to my problems from last summer. I'd ignored him that entire time, unable to even talk about what happened between us in the courtyard. But he was here now when I needed him.

"I haven't been able to shake it yet. I was sure I'd get sent home. But all of the instructors worked with me—I guess they thought I had potential."

"You do," Jacob said, not hesitating. "And you don't give yourself enough credit. You're a talented rider, Sash. You have to stop comparing yourself to everyone else. Who cares what they do? You and Charm are special— you're a team. Does *any* other rider here have a bond with her horse like you do with Charm? "

We were both quiet for a minute. I stared at my lap.

"Do you know how insecure *I* am every time I step on the track field?" Jacob asked.

I shook my head.

"I feel like I'm going to throw up before every race. The guys, even the ones on my team, talk trash about one another. I know I can't let them get inside my head when I run. You just have to block it out."

"Really?" I asked.

He nodded. "Everyone gets nervous around competition."

"Thank you," I said after a couple of minutes. "I needed to hear that."

Jacob's face changed from sympathy to anger. "And you know the only reason Jas is trash-talking you is because she's worried. If she didn't think you were worth it, she wouldn't even bother talking. She'd just ignore you."

"You think?" I asked.

"I know. She sees *you* as competition. She knows you're good, but she also knows how to get you upset. Figure out how to handle her—I know you can."

I stared to lean over to hug him, but stopped. "Thanks," I said. "You're right. I'll totally figure out a way to handle Jas."

Jacob turned his head to me and our eyes met. I took a breath and something told me I needed to go. I got up from the stairs and looked back at him as I pulled open the door. "Bye," I whispered.

I left him in the stairwell and the door shut between us. I walked out of the library, blinking in the strong sunlight.

"Hey!"

I looked up at Paige as she walked toward me, carrying her pink and purple binder and a book bag.

"Hi," I said, smiling. But I knew there was no way Paige would miss the fact that I'd been crying.

"I called you to say I was coming to study too," Paige said. "But when you didn't—" She stopped in front of me. "Omigod, what's wrong? Did something happen?"

I rolled my eyes, sighing. "Yeah. Jasmine, of course. I'll tell you, but can we go somewhere else to study? She's in the library."

"Of course!" Paige linked her arm through mine. "How about we grab a back room at the media center? We can totally reward ourselves with TV breaks while we study."

"Love it."

We walked away from the library and headed for the media center.

"So," I started. "I was walking through an aisle and I heard Jasmine talking. She was telling someone—probably one of the Belles—about how horrible I was at YENT camp."

Paige huffed. "*What?!* A: That's not true. And B: She sure spends a lot of time talking about you for someone who's not worried about you as competition."

"That's what J—" I stopped myself midsentence.

"What?"

"Nothing. I was just saying that's what Jasmine wants. You're right. Thanks," I said. "I shouldn't have even reacted to her. I'm over it now. Let her say what she wants. Who cares?"

Paige nudged me with her upper arm. "Don't just *say* that though. Believe it. You *know* Jas's game. She attacks you for not having the fancy training she had. You're a great rider, Sash, and she knows it."

I smiled at Paige. "I think after the media center, I might owe my BFF a brownie."

"The BFF will gladly accept. And BTW, if I ever call you when Jas is trashing you, just hand the phone to her. I'll take care of it." Paige gave me an I'll-totally-fight-her-for-you face.

We laughed, but I felt the familiar churn of guilt in my stomach. If I'd given away the phone when Paige had called, she would have been talking to Jacob—not Jasmine.

16

STAGE FRIGHT

I HADN'T LOOKED AT JACOB ONCE SINCE drama class had started. I wanted to, but it felt disloyal to Eric. I hadn't even told Eric anything about my Jasmine-related meltdown. I just hadn't wanted to talk about it again.

We waited on stage for Ms. Scott to give us instructions. Behind us, two banquet tables were covered with tablecloths.

"Hi, class," Ms. Scott said as she walked onstage. "I hope you're all ready for a game that's going to test your memory. I'm going to pair you up, then we'll get started."

Ms. Scott assigned partners and Heather and I ended up together.

"I'm going to own this," Heather said.

"You don't even know what the game is," I said. "You really want to say that?"

Heather snorted. "Uh, *yeah.*"

"All right," Ms. Scott said. "You're each going to take turns testing each other. One of you will walk up to the table and when your partner pulls off the tablecloth, you've got one minute to memorize the items on the table. After a minute, turn around and your partner will give you a pen and a sheet of paper. You'll have two minutes to write down as many objects as possible."

Heather and I were both going to be good at this. Years of memorizing jump courses would definitely help us here.

"Then, you and your partner will count up the items. Go to a different table and switch roles. When you've both completed the exercise, come back to center stage. This is a memory-training exercise that will be useful when you start to memorize lines. After we finish the game, we're going to go over the chapter you read last night and talk about memorization techniques that actors use."

We all took pens and paper from Ms. Scott, then wandered off to a table. Heather and I reached one of the tables first. I waved a hand at her, motioning for her to go first. "Since you're so sure you're going to win," I said, "you should go first."

Heather tossed her hair and moved in front of the table. "Tell me when to start."

I watched the clock on the wall and at just the right second, I pulled off the tablecloth. "Go!"

Heather's eyes flickered over the table and her intense gaze seemed to take in every object. *Spoon. Hair clip. Ring. Ear buds.*

"And . . . stop," I said a minute later.

Heather turned around and I handed her a pen and piece of paper. She scribbled down answers as I watched the clock for two minutes.

"Time," I said.

She handed me her paper and we started counting the items. "Twenty-six out of thirty," I said after we'd tallied them up. "Good job."

We waited for a different table to be free, then it was my turn. Heather glanced at the clock. "Okay, now," she said, pulling off the tablecloth.

I started at one end of the table and worked my way across. *Pen. Earring. CD. Sticky note. Flash drive. Scissors.* I ran through the items in my head. I said them faster and faster, trying to take in as many as I could.

"Stop," Heather said.

I turned away from the table and took the pen and paper from Heather. I wrote as fast as I could—*lip balm, keys, postcard.*

I kept writing until Heather told me to stop. Heather started counting my items. "Twenty-three, twenty-four, twenty-five . . ." She looked at me. "Twenty-five."

I shook my head. Twenty-five. One away from tying with Heather.

I pretend-bowed to her. "Nice."

Heather grinned. "As if you ever had a shot."

We walked to center stage and waited for the rest of the pairs to finish.

"How did everyone do?" Ms. Scott asked.

"I memorized more objects than my partner," Heather bragged.

By one! I wanted to interject. But whatever.

"And how did you approach memorizing the objects?" Ms. Scott asked. "Tell us your technique."

Heather paused, probably not wanting to give away her secret. "I looked at the entire table and said all of the objects in my head as fast as I could, over and over."

Ha! We totally had the same technique.

Ms. Scott knelt down to sit cross-legged on stage with

us. "Do you all think that would be a useful technique for memorizing lines?"

"Probably," Jacob said. Everyone turned to look at him. "I think repeating it helps. Maybe not as fast for lines, but I couldn't just read something one time and have it memorized."

"Me neither," I added. "I did the same thing as Heather."

We talked about technique for a few more minutes, then Ms. Scott went over the assigned reading from the last class.

"Thanks, guys," Ms. Scott said. "Remember to study for the history of theater quiz for next class. See you then."

I walked with everyone else off stage and grabbed my book bag from my seat.

"Cool class," Jacob said.

I turned to him. "Yeah. It is."

We smiled at each other.

My phone buzzed and I checked the screen—Eric. I answered. "Hey, what's up?"

"You want to meet at the Sweet Shoppe later?" he asked.

"Sash, I've gotta go," Jacob said. "Talk to you later."

I tried to cover the phone with my hand, but it was too late. Jacob stepped around me.

"Who was that?" Eric asked.

"Oh, a guy from my theater class," I said. "The Sweet Shoppe sounds great. Text me later!"

I clicked my phone shut before Eric could say another word.

"How was theater?" Callie asked in math class. "It sounds like such a cool elective. If Website Design hadn't been offered, I definitely would have taken it."

"It's cool. We play lots of improv games."

"Awesome," Callie said. She smoothed her dark purple skirt with black swirls. "That sounds like so much fun."

"Totally," I said. "It doesn't even feel like a class. It's a good break considering all of the work we have in every other class."

Callie nodded and pulled out her assignment notebook. "Ugh. Seriously. I can barely cram all of today's homework into the *giant* space that's supposed to hold all of it."

"Mine's full too. I know what we'll be doing all night."

Callie frowned and then looked up at me. "Want to

come over to Orchard's common room tonight? We can do homework together."

"Definitely," I said. "That'll make it slightly less painful."

Ms. Utz walked into the room and started taking attendance. She was so tall, she made the podium look a foot high.

"Let's start by having a few of you go up to the board and work out a few sample problems," Ms. Utz said. "Sasha, Kelly, and Devyn, please go up to the board."

I slid out of my desk and went up to the whiteboard. I tried to pay attention as Ms. Utz read out the problems we needed to solve, but I couldn't stop analyzing my latest lie. Had Eric recognized Jacob's voice? And when did a bunch of little white lies add to up one huge disaster?

17

CAN YOU SAY "PARANOID"?

LATER THAT AFTERNOON, I TACKED UP CHARM for our lesson. My sweaty fingers struggled to tighten his girth. *Calm down,* I told myself. I couldn't mess up another lesson just because I felt intimidated. That would be giving Jasmine exactly what she wanted. I'd earned my spot on the team and I was going to work hard to keep it.

"We've got this, right, Charm?" He craned his neck around to look at me. His big brown eyes were calm and it made me feel better to remember that he'd be in the arena with me. I brushed a stalk of straw off my black breeches and put on my helmet.

I walked Charm down the arena, passing Julia and Alison along the way. The girls led their horses down the aisle. Alison gave me a small smile and Julia stared ahead, not looking at me. I edged Charm out of the way so Trix and Sunstruck could squeeze past us. I felt for both girls *and* their horses. Charm would pine away if I couldn't ride him for months. Trix and Sunstruck had to miss Julia and Alison.

Charm and I warmed up in the arena. Within minutes, Jasmine and Heather trotted Phoenix and Aristocrat inside. I kept focus, refusing to look at either girl. Mr. Conner came into the arena and we lined up in front of him. I already knew that today was a dressage lesson because Mr. Conner had e-mailed us a test to familiarize ourselves with the movements before class.

"Hi, girls," Mr. Conner said. "Before we start, I wanted to let you know that I'll be videotaping a lesson to share with Mr. Nicholson next week. This lesson won't different from any other, so there's no reason to be nervous."

I blinked. Yeah, no reason to be nervous except that if one of us messed up and got thrown off the YENT, it would be so humiliating that changing schools wouldn't even be enough. Hello, homeschooling.

"As for today, as long as everyone's horses are warmed up," Mr. Conner said, "you're each going to perform the dressage test that was e-mailed to you. I did not expect anyone to memorize it in that short amount of time—I just wanted to familiarize you with it. Heather, you may ride first."

Jasmine and I moved our horses to the side of the arena. Heather rode Aristocrat to the arena's exit and waited for a signal from Mr. Conner to start. They looked confident and together before they even started.

"Enter at a medium walk, halt at X, and salute," Mr. Conner said.

Heather did and Mr. Conner took her through the rest of the test. She and Aristocrat were almost in perfect synch from move to move.

"Exit at A at a free walk," Mr. Conner said. Heather did and rode Aristocrat back to Jas and me.

"Nice," I said. "Aristocrat looked great during the circles."

"Thanks," Heather said.

Jas rolled her eyes and looked at me. "When did *you* become a dressage expert?"

Mr. Conner walked up to us, still marking on his clipboard. He finally looked up at Heather. "Aristocrat's gaits looked smooth," he said. "Your circles were great. I'd like you to work more on impulsion."

"I will," Heather said. "His hind legs weren't as engaged as they should have been."

"I agree," Mr. Conner said. "Watch a few United States Equestrian Team DVDs and pay attention to how the riders encourage their horses to move forward with energy."

Mr. Conner looked at me. "You're up, Sasha. Please exit the arena and wait for my signal."

I tried to breathe as I rode Charm through the exit, then turned him back to face the arena. Mr. Conner instructed me to enter, and Charm and I started the same test Heather had just completed.

Charm was supple under me and I felt him relax with each move. The hours in YENT camp that we'd practiced dressage were paying off. We moved from marker to marker, listening to Mr. Conner as he called out the moves.

"Working trot to *C*," Mr. Conner called.

Charm and I completed the last twenty-meter circle, trotted down the centerline, slowed to a walk, and halted. Charm stopped the second I asked him to. I saluted Mr. Conner and left the arena. Charm trotted over to rejoin Aristocrat and Phoenix. The mock test had been one of our best and I couldn't wait to tell Callie—she was one of the best dressage riders at school. She was going to be superproud.

"That was nice, Sasha," Mr. Conner said. "Where did Charm feel strongest to you?"

"During the working trot," I said. "He was on the bit and listening to me."

Mr. Conner nodded. "I'd say the same. Good ride." He marked something on his clipboard.

Jas leaned over to me. "I'm about to make your test look even more pathetic than it actually was," she said.

"Go for it," I said.

Jas cued Phoenix forward and I watched, knowing my test had been good, but Jas was stronger in dressage.

Heather and I were silent as we watched Jas ride. Phoenix changed gaits the second Jas asked him to, flowed through every circle and halted crisply when it was time for her to salute. He stood still, not even flicking an ear while he waited for a signal from Jas.

"Well done," Mr. Conner said. "I'd like to see Phoenix just a touch less submissive, though. He needs to move with more confidence and freedom."

"Yes, sir," Jasmine said. "I'll practice that with him." Jas patted Phoenix's neck and the gray lowered his head, responding to her touch.

"Good job, everyone," Mr. Conner said. "You've all impressed me today. I can see great changes in your dressage movements since YENT camp. I'll see you tomorrow."

He left the arena and I dismounted, smiling to myself.

Charm and I had sooo needed that lesson to go as well as it had.

I cooled him out and groomed him. He stood quietly on crossties while I mucked his stall and refilled his water bucket. Mike or Doug had given him a fresh flake of hay while I'd been in class.

I released him into his stall and latched the door shut. I leaned over the door, putting my arms on top and resting my chin on my arms while I watched Charm take a drink, and then move to his hay net.

"You were a total dressage star," I said. "I can't wait to tell Callie."

Eric would be happy for me too. He knew I struggled with dressage.

"Bye, boy," I told Charm. "I'll see you tomorrow."

I gathered his tack and walked to the tack room. I could hear laughter through the door before I'd even pushed it open. Inside, Rachel and two of her friends—I could never remember their names—were leaning against an empty saddle rack, grinning at Eric. He looked up, sponge in hand as he scrubbed the cantle of Luna's saddle.

"Hey, Sasha," he said.

"Hi," I said, smiling at him and nodding at Rachel and her friends. One had braces and the other had short brown hair with blond highlights. They were always following Eric around and practically drooling over him. But there was no way I was going to let it bother me.

"How was your lesson?" Rachel asked.

"Fine, thanks," I said.

Rachel stepped aside as I plopped Charm's saddle onto his saddle rack.

"Eric, do you need help or anything?" Rachel asked. "We can totally clean tack, too."

Before Eric could respond, I turned around to look at Rachel. "I think he's got it. Don't you have your own tack or horses to take care of?"

I regretted it the second it came out of my mouth.

Rachel's eyes locked with mine for a second before she took a tiny step back. "Yeah. I guess we do. See you."

She and her friends shuffled out of the room and I shook my head, letting out a slow breath. I put Charm's bridle on the hook and turned to find Eric with his arms folded.

"What was *that* about?" he asked. "You okay?"

I ducked my head, knowing I'd been wrong. Rachel was definitely annoying, but she was harmless. Eric would never go for her—ever.

"Sorry," I said. "I'm tired and I guess I just overreacted. I'm fine, really."

Eric walked over and wrapped his arms around me. I leaned into his hug, squeezing him.

"That," I said, "was exactly what I needed."

Eric ran his hands down my arms. "I know. Things have been bad this week. But remember how overwhelmed I was when I first came to Canterwood? And you too? It *will* get better."

I forced a smile. "I know. It will."

When I figure out a way to stop lying to you and everyone else.

"I've got to go," I said. "Callie and I are studying in Orchard."

"Sounds like my night. But I'll be in Blackwell with a couple of guys from my floor."

Eric squeezed my hand and smiled at me as I walked to the door.

I left him in the tack room, cleaning Luna's saddle, and headed for Winchester. Distracted, I almost walked into a bench. *Stop it,* I told myself. Rachel was nothing to worry about. She was a seventh grader with a crush. Eric would never cheat on me. I was just exhausted and paranoid from trying to keep up with my own lies. I obviously couldn't trust anyone else because *I* was doing so much lying.

18
DEFINE "TRUST"

CALLIE AND I NEEDED TWO TABLES IN ORCHARD to hold all of our books, papers, folders, and notes. I'd always liked visiting Orchard's common room. The walls were painted a light cranberry and trimmed with oatmeal-colored paint. The colors made the room feel sophisticated—like a college hangout.

"This," Callie said, "is ridiculous." She shook her head at our mess.

"Totally. The teachers have lost it. I mean, I don't even know where to start."

"But at least that's been the only bad part about school starting," Callie said, smiling. "We knew there would be tons of homework and we'll get it done. Everything else has been so awesome. I missed you and Jacob so much over the summer and it's been so much fun hanging out. It was hard to be away from Jacob for a whole summer."

"I get it. And that's great," I said, flipping to a clean sheet of paper. "Is he superbusy too?"

"Yeah, we have to coordinate schedules just to get coffee. It's so wrong."

"Same thing with Eric and me. Our phones are having the relationship right now. At least I get to see him once in a while at the stable."

Callie giggled. "How's riding? Tell me about it. We've barely had a chance to talk about that."

"It's hard," I said. "I'm just trying to focus on myself and not worry about Heather and Jasmine. If I could stop worrying about them, things would be so much easier."

"Absolutely. That's your thing—you're good and you don't give yourself enough credit. You can absolutely compete with those girls. You're going to *kill* at shows."

There wasn't a hint of insincerity in Callie's voice.

"Thanks." I smiled. "How are your lessons going?"

"Pretty well," Callie said. "You would have been so proud of Eric and me today."

"What happened?"

Callie uncapped her Zebra highlighter. "We worked on jumping in the outdoor arena today. Mr. Conner set up a bunch of verticals of increasing height. We both got called out by Mr. Conner for having the best form when we jumped."

"Niiice." I raised my palm for a high five. "Eric didn't tell me about that."

"He was cool about it," Callie said. "But I couldn't stop smiling after Mr. Conner said it to me. I told Eric that he was making me look bad."

I sighed quietly. Callie and Eric—my best friend and boyfriend—were having fun together and I was miserable on my own team.

I flipped to the right chapter for history before glancing over at Callie. "So . . . do you and Eric talk a lot? Like, before or after class?"

Callie shrugged and wrote her name on her math worksheet. "Sometimes. You know how it is—there's not really much time to talk. Everyone's rushing around to get to the arena on time."

"Yeah," I said.

Callie glanced over at me. "You don't care that we're talking, right? Do you?"

"No, no!" I said. "I don't care at all." My voice got squeaky and I *knew* Callie would think I was lying. I didn't care if they talked all day—I just hated that they were building a friendship because if they ever found out about my lies, that friendship would be ruined too.

Callie looked down at the table. "It's just . . . I thought we were past that. After what happened with Jacob, you still don't trust me with Eric?"

I dropped my pen and reached across the table to touch her arm. "Of *course* I do, Callie. I know it sounded that way, but it wasn't what I meant at all. I promise."

Callie stared at me for a minute, playing with her silver hoop earring. "Okay. Because you know I'd never do that again. *Ever.* I'm just so glad we're best friends again. I'd never risk messing that up. And . . . I'm really happy with Jacob."

Guilt. Guiltguiltguilt. "Just forget I said that. We *are* best friends. I don't care at all if you talk to Eric. Really."

Callie smiled. "Okay. And finally, right? No secrets— nothing. It's a good feeling."

I nodded and we went back to our homework. A few minutes later my phone buzzed. I leaned over and opened the phone.

Hope 2day's lesson went btr.

Jacob.

I snapped the phone shut and took a breath before I sat up.

Right. No more secrets.

19

ADMIT WHAT?

AT THE CAFETERIA, I DUG INTO MY MAC AND cheese and then moved onto my burger. Paige had a teacher meeting and was missing this lunch period. Eric was running late from class and had texted that he'd be late and to start lunch without him.

Someone sat across from me and I looked up, expecting to see Callie. But it was Jacob.

"What are you doing?" I asked.

"Come on," Jacob said. "We *are* allowed to talk." He brushed his hair out of his eyes and folded his arms on top of the table.

"Jacob, stop it. Eric's going to be here any second and I really don't want him to see us talking."

"Because he'd be jealous?" Jacob's eyes were on my face.

"No," I said, slowly. "Because . . ."

I couldn't finish my sentence. Truth: Eric would be annoyed at Jacob for talking to me, but he wouldn't be mad at me. Truer truth: If Eric saw Jacob and me talking, I wondered if he'd be able to sense that I was confused about my feelings for Jacob.

"Because," I started again. "I hate coming to lunch and feeling like I have to hide from you. You keep coming up to me even though I asked you not to."

My voice had an angry edge. I wanted Jacob to go.

But instead of getting up and walking away, he leaned closer. "You're not mad at me," he said, his voice quiet. "You just hate this situation."

I looked down.

"You hate that you're confused about how you feel. I know that you . . ." Jacob paused. ". . . *like* Eric, but you also like me. And you don't want to admit it because it would make you feel like the worst girlfriend and an awful best friend."

My ears pounded and my face flushed. There wasn't an ounce of question in his voice.

"Jacob," I said. "That's not at all what—"

Jacob shook his head. "Stop lying. If you can't tell me that you like me, at least consider admitting it to yourself. Then maybe you'll be able to figure out what to do."

I realized I hadn't taken a breath in a while and I gulped in air. I wanted to tell Jacob that I was confused. That I still liked Eric. And that I couldn't hurt Callie. I looked down at my plate, then back at Jacob.

"You need to go," I said. "Before Eric gets here. Please."

Jacob took a deep breath, then nodded. "Okay. But you're going to hurt them more in the end by lying to yourself."

"I am *not* lying," I heard myself say. "I like Eric. You like Callie. And the only thing I'm lying about is what *you* did—confessing that you still liked me. And you have *no* idea how much that's complicated everything."

Jacob's eyes focused on mine. "I'm sorry I made things weird for you, but I had to tell you how I felt. I do like Callie. But you and I never got a chance. I want that."

He got up and left the cafeteria. I stared at the doorway, not knowing what I wanted. Did I want Jacob to come back and argue with me again? Not show up for lunch again? I didn't know. But I did know that he was wrong about one thing—my lies were protecting everyone, not hurting them.

Callie and Eric were never going to find out, especially not after I was working so hard to keep it from them.

Callie would never be hurt by what Jacob had said because I'd never tell her. Eric would never know that Jacob and I had been talking and no one would ever know that I'd wondered if I was with the right guy.

Eric's it, I told myself. *Put it to rest.*

Eric appeared in the doorway and scanned the caf for me. I waved and he smiled and got in the lunch line. I watched him the entire way through the line—and seeing him only reconfirmed my decision. I liked Eric so much and he had always been there for me. Jacob needed to leave me alone.

Eric sat down, sighing.

"What's wrong?" I asked.

"Nothing," he said. "I just saw Jacob in the hallway and he just gave me this *look.* I try to be cool with that guy, but then he acts like a total jerk."

I pressed my lips together—trying to say the right thing. "Maybe it wasn't directed at you. He could just be having a bad day or something."

Eric shrugged. "Why? Did he say something to you before I got here?"

Yes. Only that he still wants me back.

"No," I said. "I saw him, but he didn't talk to me. He looked kind of mad, so that's why I said it probably wasn't about you."

The lie slipped out so easily. I wanted to smack myself in the face. I could have told him that I *had* talked to Jacob without going into detail about our conversation. But instead, I'd lied about the whole thing.

Eric nodded and took a bite of his meatball sub. "Okay. Let's not talk about Jacob anymore." He smiled and offered me a French fry. "Tell me about health class with Utz. I *wish* I'd gotten her for that class."

I laughed, glad to talk about *anything* else. "You're *so* missing the best class ever," I said. "It's just been general health stuff so far. But soon, she's going to be prepping us to start CPR on the dummies. I already know that's going to be amaaazing."

Eric grinned.

"I can't wait till she teaches you the Heimlich," Eric said. "I just hope she's never had to really save anyone from choking. She'd lock them into some crazy wrestling move and probably break their ribs."

"So true. Maybe choking would be a less painful way to go," I teased. "Instead of being crushed by Utz."

We laughed and joked until the end of the period.

I looked down at Mr. Conner from atop Charm's back, waiting for instruction. Heather, Jasmine, and I had just led our horses outside and mounted. I patted Charm's neck as Mr. Conner consulted his clipboard, then looked up at us.

"We'll be doing cross-country today," Mr. Conner said.

Charm's ears went forward. Charm and I *loved* cross-country. Plus, today was the perfect day to be out on the course. It was supercloudy and breezy—as if it could pour at any second—a welcome change from the lessons we'd sweated through.

Mr. Conner's eyes stayed on me for a second and he smiled. "Sasha, you're up first. We're going to take a new abbreviated course that was just set up in the field. It's a basic course and the jumps are fairly simple—we're just using it as a starter for the season before we go back to the regular course. You've all looked over the diagram I e-mailed last night, right?"

We nodded. The course wasn't too long or complicated enough that it required us to walk it before riding, but Mr. Conner had sent us a course map so we'd know where to go.

"Heather and Jasmine," Mr. Conner continued, "I want you both to watch Sasha's technique. She knows how to get the best out of Charm—when to push him and when to hold him back."

I tried not to grin. Mr. Conner rarely gave out compliments and when he did, it was a big deal.

"Let's go," Mr. Conner said.

We started toward the course and Charm's pace quickened with every stride. When we reached the start, Mr. Conner turned to me. "There aren't any surprises out there, so there's no need to worry about not having walked the course. You'll be able to see each jump ahead of time. There's nothing you or Charm haven't encountered before. All right?"

I nodded. "Okay."

Mr. Conner patted Charm's shoulder. "Whenever you're ready."

I sat deep in the saddle and let Charm into a walk. He broke into a trot a few strides away from the group. I circled him, warming him up for a few seconds, and then let him into a canter. I couldn't help but smile. This was our shot to redeem ourselves after a round of bad lessons.

"All right," I said to Charm. "Go!"

I gave him more rein and he moved into a canter over the grass. I got him collected before pointing him in the direction of the first brush jump. Charm, controlled and focused, cantered up to the brush and at the right time, I leaned forward and rose out of the saddle. Charm tucked his knees and jumped into the air, his body arching over the brush. He landed on the other side.

This was how Charm and I worked together. We should have been doing this since the first YENT lesson of the year.

I relaxed in the saddle and gave Charm another bit of rein. We reached another brush fence, a couple of inches higher . . . Charm's takeoff was perfect.

We landed and had to canter uphill to reach the next jump. I slowed Charm's pace and adjusted my position, leaning forward slightly to prevent myself from slipping back in the saddle.

I tried to hold my focus, but my mind started to wander and I flashed back to lunch. All day, I'd been sure that Eric hadn't suspected me of lying when I'd told him that I hadn't talked to Jacob. But what if he found out? What if he'd seen me talking to Jacob and pretended to see Jacob for the first time in the hallway?

Oh, stop it, I told myself. I was being ridiculous. Eric wasn't like that—he would have said something if he'd seen me talking to Jacob. All of my lies were making me paranoid. But now I felt like I couldn't stop lying. If I did, everything would unravel and—

I almost flipped over Charm's shoulder as he slid to

a stop in front of a log jump. My chest slammed into Charm's neck and I lost a stirrup.

"Omigod," I said aloud. *Way to lose focus!* I hadn't even realized where we were on the course. Charm could have rammed into the log and been hurt.

Charm backed out of his braced pose and straightened, shaking his head.

"Charm," I said. "I'm so sorry."

I readjusted my feet in the stirrups and rubbed Charm's neck. Turning him away from the obstacle, I urged him into a canter and circled him twice before pointing him back at the jump. Charm took it this time without a pause and I forced myself to stay focused.

The breeze picked up and whipped Charm's mane into the air. Clouds shifted overhead and blocked the sun. The next jump, a wooden gate, was seconds away. I counted down the strides—determined not to make another mistake. Charm reached the gate and jumped into the air, and I moved into the two-point position. I raised my hands along Charm's crest, giving him rein but not enough to let him pull me forward.

We made it over the gate and took the rest of the course without a problem. I trotted Charm back to the group, trying not to look at Jasmine or Heather. Jasmine snorted under her breath when I eased Charm to a halt between Phoenix and Aristocrat. My whole body burned with embarrassment. Charm and I always killed at cross country. But we kept blowing lesson after lesson. Correction: *I* kept blowing lesson after lesson.

"Sasha," Mr. Conner said. "You started strong and then something happened at the log jump. Tell us about that."

I wanted to turn Charm and gallop away from Heather and Jasmine. Fessing up to my mistakes in front of them was the worst. But I had to—Mr. Conner was waiting.

"We did well over the first jump and I got confident," I said. "I let my attention wander, thinking the rest of the course was going to be easy."

"You went on autopilot," Mr. Conner said.

I nodded. "It was a huge mistake. I know you have to pay attention every second on cross-country, and I didn't."

Mr. Conner stared at me, but his expression wasn't angry—it looked more like concern. "It was a dangerous error, but you did recover. I want to reiterate to all of you how crucial it is to focus not only during cross-country, but also during every phase of riding."

We all nodded.

"Jasmine, you may ride now," Mr. Conner said.

Jas cantered away from us almost before Mr. Conner finished his sentence. She and Phoenix took every jump as if they were inches high. Phoenix stayed collected and relaxed under Jas's hands and she didn't rush him once. Jas had been the worst at rushing fences and pushing Phoenix too hard. But since she'd made the YENT, she'd made an effort to become a softer rider.

"Excellent, Jasmine," Mr. Conner said. "Your timing was perfect."

Jasmine beamed at him, then turned to smirk at me when he signaled Heather to go.

Aristocrat and Heather were a near-unbeatable team and they showed it on the course. Heather had a finesse that Jas lacked and she knew how to get the best out of Aristocrat. She was a cooler rider than I was because she was somehow able to turn off her emotions when she rode. Or, if she was thinking about anything that was bothering her, she didn't let it show when she rode.

Mr. Conner talked through each of our strengths and weaknesses, then dismissed class. I dismounted and spent extra time cooling Charm. I groomed him in his stall, hiding from everyone in the main aisle. I didn't know what was wrong with me! I knew all of my lies were in the best interest of protecting my friends, but I couldn't stop stressing about any of them finding out the truth.

I leaned against Charm's shoulder, letting my weight rest against him. Charm, seeming to know I needed someone, didn't even go his hay net. He stood still and let me rest on him.

"Sasha?" Mr. Conner's head appeared over the door. "Let's talk in my office for a minute."

"Okay." I could barely get out the word. I latched Charm's stall door shut and walked behind Mr. Conner, feeling as if I was in a daze. This was it. He was going to tell me I'd messed up too many times to be on the YENT. He'd say there was no way he'd be able to help me improve enough to impress Mr. Nicholson when he taped one of our riding lessons.

Mr. Conner motioned me inside ahead of him and I took a seat in front of his desk. He shut the door, sat at the black leather chair behind his giant desk, and folded his hands on top of his desk. He looked up at me.

"Sasha, I just wanted to talk to you for a minute. First, I want you to know how much I believe in your talent as a rider. I'm proud that you're on the YENT and I know how important it is to you."

I swallowed. I couldn't say anything.

"Is there anything going on at home or with classes that you'd like to talk about?" Mr. Conner asked. His brown eyes were kind as he looked at me. "I'm here if you need to talk—it doesn't have to be riding-related."

I shifted in my seat. "Thanks, but everything's fine with school and at home." I stared down at my clenched hands and then looked up at him. "I thought you asked me in here to tell me that I was off the team."

"Sasha, no," Mr. Conner said quickly. "Not at all. I've just noticed that you've seemed stressed since school resumed. I know it's difficult to get back into a routine after summer break is over. But if there is anything going on that's affecting your riding, please know that you can talk to me."

I let out a breath.

"I've been trying to find the balance of being back to school, seeing my friends, handling homework . . . just normal stuff," I said. "But nothing's wrong. I promise I won't let it affect my riding again. I know the YENT is a huge opportunity and I'd never waste it."

Mr. Conner shook his head. "You're not wasting anything, Sasha. I just want you to take some pressure off yourself, to block out whoever you think is your competition, and to learn everything you can from this experience."

Mr. Conner knew I'd been watching Jas and Heather. Somehow, he was able to tell that I'd been paying more attention to them than to my own riding.

"I will," I promised. "I'm going to get everything under control. I'm sorry I lost focus."

Mr. Conner smiled. "You'll have plenty of time to correct that. We've got a long competition season ahead of us."

I sat back in my chair and nodded. He had *no* idea how long the year already felt.

20

JUST GIVE ME
SOMETHING

WHEN I WALKED INTO MY ROOM, PAIGE jumped up and hurried to shove a bunch of papers into a yellow folder. She turned, grinned at me, and held the folder behind her back.

"Sasha!" she said. "Hi!"

I folded my arms, pretend-staring her down. "What's in the folder, Parker?"

Paige shrugged. "Oh, you know. Like, homework. Boring stuff you wouldn't want to see."

"Really? 'Cause I *love* boring stuff of the homework variety."

Paige and I held each other's gaze for a second, then started laughing. "You're not getting one peek at your birthday party plans. Not one."

I walked over to sit at the edge of my bed and pull off my riding boots. "Nothing?" I clapped a hand to my chest. "It's only Tuesday. Give me something to survive till Friday."

Holding the folder away from me, Paige opened it and thumbed through the papers. "Okay, okay," she said. "I'll be supergenerous and tell you the guest list."

"Oooh, yay!"

Paige pulled out a light pink sheet of paper. "All right. We've got . . . Callie, Eric, Jacob, Heather, Julia, Alison, Nicole, Troy, Ben, Andy, Annabella, Suichin, and Ryan. They've all RSVP'd yes. Pretty awesome, huh?"

"Very!" I said, smiling. I didn't want Paige to see how I really felt. "It's going to be great 'cause you're planning it."

Paige grinned. "Duh." Then she stared at me for a second. "Hey. You okay?"

"Totally," I said. "Just thinking about one person not on that list."

Good cover, I thought to myself. I'd never tell Paige that her guest list was probably going to give me hives before the end of the week.

Paige scrunched up her face. "I know—Jasmine. I wanted to talk to you about that. She lives on this floor, and since we're holding the party in the common room, she's *going* to show up."

"I know. So do we just invite her instead of letting her crash?"

Nodding, Paige put down the folder. "That's what I'd do. Fingers crossed that she'll just think it's going to be an uberlame party and not even show up."

"True," I said. "Really, why would she want to come to my party anyway? But go ahead and invite her."

"Speaking of Jas . . . how was riding with her?" Paige asked. "Was she awful?"

"No, *I* was," I mumbled.

"What? No, you weren't." Paige made a don't-talk-like-that-about-yourself face.

"It's true. I messed up during cross-country and, ugh, so mortifying, Mr. Conner asked me to his office to talk."

Paige sat on her bed, looking at me. "What did he say?"

"That he knows I'm trying and if I needed to talk him about anything, I could."

"That was nice of him," Paige said. "He wasn't saying your riding wasn't up to YENT level or anything."

"No, but he got that I was too focused on Heather

and Jas. I mean, he didn't come right out and say it, but he knew."

"He *is* Mr. Conner." Paige smiled.

I smiled back. "I know. I messed up today, but I've got it now. I don't care about Heather or Jas!"

"Good!" Paige nodded and went back to work at her desk and I headed for the shower.

Leaning my back against the closed bathroom door, I rubbed my eyes with my fingers. I'd covered my nerves about the party with the story about riding, which *had* been true. Paige was planning a blowout party that would be amazing. But I felt so guilty that everyone was coming for me and I was such a liar. Plus, what if Eric and Jacob got into it again and Jacob told him the truth?

The whole party—no, my life—would be ruined. I'd just have to make sure I didn't make one mistake.

21

GIRL TALK

ON WEDNESDAY AFTERNOON, CALLIE AND I scanned the chalkboard with the Sweet Shoppe's specials of the day.

"Um, we're *so* getting frozen yogurt," Callie said. "They've got strawberry-mango today."

"Done," I said. "Large, of course."

Callie grinned. "Natch."

We got our orders and picked out a table in the back of the shop, where it was quiet. We started to eat and I smiled to myself, thinking how good this felt. Callie and me hanging out with no pressure and zero weirdness. Maybe things were finally going to be back to normal.

Callie stuck her spoon into her yogurt and leaned

BURKHART

forward. "So, did you hear the latest about Julia and Ben?"

"Nooo! What?" My spoon hovered in the air halfway between my cup and my mouth.

"They just got back together," Callie said. "They're keeping it on the DL, though."

"Why? No one cares if they're back together." I took a bite of yogurt.

"You'd think, but I heard Julia telling Alison that she's sure Jas will try to steal Ben if she knows they're together just because she hates Julia so much."

"Maybe," I said. "But we've all got to stop being afraid to go public with our boyfriends." I laughed. "It's just wrong!"

Callie raised her spoon and we touched them together. "Agreed! And we really need to work on said boyfriends. The hating-each-other thing is getting old."

"Totally. It would be so much easier for all of us to hang out if they'd chill."

Callie rolled her eyes. "Jacob can be *so* stubborn. He just won't get over his thing with Eric. They both need to grow up."

"You think?" I smiled at her. "But no matter what—even

if they never even look at each other again—we're still best friends. They'll have to deal."

Callie nodded. "Yeah! I mean, we can have boyfriends, but it can't take up all of our best-friend time."

I smiled. Callie sounded more like herself than she had in months. She wasn't clinging to Jacob and she wanted to do things with me. We were gossiping and joking like we used to.

I took my time eating my yogurt and so did Callie. We got into a long and very important conversation about whether or not Amberlynn, a ninth grader, had made the right decision to get bangs.

"You could totally do them with your face shape," Callie said. "They'd look amazing."

I touched my hair. "It's too wavy. I'd be attached to my flatiron."

Callie giggled. "I can imagine you keeping it in your purse and straightening your bangs in between classes with one of those portable ones."

"But you could do bangs," I said. "Your hair is straight. Sideswept bangs would be pretty."

"I might," Callie said. "And whatever. If I don't like them, they'll grow out."

I ate a few more bites of yogurt, then my phone buzzed. I checked it.

"A reminder from my calendar," I explained. "I've got to tell Livvie that I'm going to stay with Paige during fall break."

"You guys are going to have sooo much fun," Callie said. "My parents are excited that I'm coming home for a week—I'm totally taking advantage of them." She grinned. "They're going to take me to all of my fave local restaurants and Mom will probably take me shopping."

"I love the way you think," I said. "I know Paige and I will do some serious shopping in Manhattan. She was telling me about sample sales and how you almost have to fight people to get the good stuff because the prices are so awesome."

"If you see anything I'd like, you better snag it for me," Callie said.

"Duh."

We gossiped and talked about what to look for at the sample sales—purses and shoes—for another hour before hugging and starting back toward our dorms. I wrapped my arms across my chest as I walked. Maybe I'd been making too big a deal out of everything over the past week and a half.

22

WISE ADVICE
FROM A LIAR

PAIGE AND I CLIMBED INTO OUR BEDS THAT
night and I reached to flick off the light.

"You've been quiet since you got back from the Sweet
Shoppe," Paige said. "Everything cool between you and
Callie?"

"Totally," I said, pausing. I finally didn't have to lie for
once. "We had fun."

"But something's been going on since school started,"
Paige said. "I'm your BFF—I *do* notice these things."

I knew I wasn't going to get away with the I'm-
completely-fine-and-stop-asking routine with Paige much
longer. We *did* live together.

"The only weird thing with Callie is the YENT," I
said. "She's happy I made it, but I don't know how much

to talk to her about it. I don't want to make her feel bad that she's missing it. But it would be obvious if I didn't talk about it at all."

Paige made a sympathetic face. "That's true. But you know Callie's proud of you. I'm sure it's okay if you talk about the YENT like you guys talked about riding last year."

"I know," I said. "I'm probably reading into it more than I should. Things are great with us and I don't want it to disappear."

Paige tossed her small purple star pillow at me. "It's not going to disappear. Everything's going to be fine. And let's talk about something happy before we go to sleep— like your party."

"A most excellent idea," I said, grinning.

"It's going to be so amazing," Paige said. "And I'm excited, too, because . . ."

I looked at her. She blushed and covered her face with her pillow.

"Because some guy you *might* like named Ryan is going to be there?" I asked. "Could that possibly be it?"

"Yesss," Paige said, her voice muffled by her pillow.

"I'm glad he'll be there," I said. "It's another no-pressure-of-being-alone type of situation where you guys can hang out."

Paige removed the pillow. "Right. And that just makes me feel more comfortable. I know! I know! I'm such a dork. I like Ryan a lot, but I'm totally intimidated by the idea of a date with him."

"There's nothing wrong with that," I said. "Please. You could go on fifty group dates before you went out with him by yourself. Whatever makes you comfortable."

Paige raised herself up on her elbow. "Be real. No guy's going to do group dates forever. Your party will be it and then if he really likes me, he'll want us to go out . . . alone."

"But you could be 'alone' at the Sweet Shoppe. Or the movies. Or a picnic in the courtyard. There are plenty of people around and you won't feel nervous about being on a date-date."

It felt good to be the one giving Paige advice for once. I was always going to her with a zillion questions, but I actually had experience with boys—not that I'd had a perfect score in that arena.

Paige nodded. "That's true. But I really like him. Why don't I want to go out with him by myself yet?"

I thought for a second. "Maybe you're just scared to take that step. But you don't have to. Not till you're ready. If he has a problem with doing what you want, then drop him."

Paige grinned. "Wise advice from the girl with the amazing boyfriend."

I turned off the light. "Yeah. An amazing boyfriend."

And I was doing absolutely everything necessary to keep him.

23

¿HABLA ESPAÑOL?
APPARENTLY NOT

I WALKED INTO SPANISH CLASS, FLIPPING through my assignment notebook. There, in purple, was *presentation abt self* in Thursday's assignments due box. And I didn't have it. I'd forgotten all about it—something I'd never done. But I'd been thinking about so many other things! I tried to imagine telling Señora Perez that I hadn't done the homework because I'd been distracted by my boyfriend and ex–almost-boyfriend. *Yeah, that would go over well.*

I slid into my seat and yanked my Spanish book from my bag. I flipped to the dictionary in the back and grabbed a clean sheet of paper, tearing off the corner by mistake. I checked the clock as students filed into the classroom. Class didn't start for five minutes—I could come up with something.

Hola, I wrote. *Me llamo Sasha.*

"Hey," Eric said, sitting down beside me.

I kept flipping through the dictionary. "Hi," I said. "Forgot about the presentation so I'm writing it now."

"Ohhh. Sorry. Go ahead."

Eric left me alone to finish. I managed to scribble three more sentences about myself before Señora Perez walked into the room. She never wore anything but skirts or dresses and today wasn't any different. She'd paired a flowy brown skirt with a collared white shirt. Eric and I'd debated about whether or not she actually owned any pants.

"Buenas tardes," she said. "Let's get the presentations out of the way first. I hope you're all prepared." She looked around the class and everyone ducked their heads—no one wanted to go first.

"Sasha," Señora Perez said.

My head dipped even more.

"You may go first," she finished.

I looked at Eric who smiled at me. *You got it,* he mouthed.

I slid my paper off my desk and stood. At least I'd be done and then I wouldn't have to worry about it the rest of class. Standing in front of class, I stared down at my red ballet flats before looking up at everyone. My eyes wandered to Eric and he gave me a reassuring smile.

"*Hola,*" I started. "*Me llamo Sasha. Soy de los Estados Unidos.*"

My face burned. I was going to fail this assignment. Saying I was from the United States was so lame! I hadn't even narrowed it down to Connecticut.

"I . . ." I looked at my paper and froze.

I locked eyes with Eric and he looked as if he wanted to jump up, grab my paper, and finish my speech for me. He was gazing at me with such empathy that it almost made things worse.

"Keep going, Sasha," Señora Perez encouraged. "Don't worry about pronunciation for every word. Just try."

I could do this. I knew how to say that I rode horses.

"*Yo monto . . . burros,*" I blurted out.

Oh.

My.

God.

I just said I rode *donkeys*!! WHY?! Charm would be *majorly* insulted that I'd called him a donkey!

The entire class smirked. My skin burned with embarrassment. This was the worst class of my life! I'd never said anything that dumb before.

"Class," Señora Perez reprimanded. "Sasha, go ahead."

I started over, this time saying that I rode horses and was an only child before I stumbled back to my seat.

Brilliant. A-plus.

"Thank you, Sasha," Señora Perez said.

She marked something in her grade book and I hurried back to my seat, fighting the urge to bang my forehead against the desktop.

Everyone else did their presentations and Señora Perez gave us our homework for the next day. I was the first one out of the classroom with Eric close behind me.

"Hey," he called, taking my arm. "You messed up just a little. You pulled it off anyway."

I groaned. "I said I rode *donkeys*! Who says that?! Omigod."

"You, apparently," Eric teased, smiling. "C'mon. It's over. No one will even remember tomorrow. You'll be prepared for the next one."

I leaned into him as we walked down the hallway and he put an arm around my waist. "Ugh. I know you're right— it just doesn't feel that way yet."

"It will soon. And you have way better things to think about," Eric said. He looked down at me. "Your party is tomorrow! I can't wait to celebrate your birthday with you."

I felt tension slip out of my body. Eric's arm was warm and snug around me in the chilly air-conditioned hallway. Eric pulled open the heavy door to the stairwell and motioned me ahead of him. It was empty inside. With a slight shake of my head, I realized I'd been spending a lot of time in stairwells lately.

The door shut behind us and we were alone on the landing.

"We really need to see each other more," I said. "We haven't had much time to be together outside of class."

Eric's brown eyes flickered over my face and he placed a warm hand on my back. "We will. Starting tomorrow. We'll go to your party and then we'll have to do something this weekend. Deal?"

"Deal."

Eric was so close to me that, for a second, I was sure I could hear *his* heart beating. He leaned closer and kissed me. Eric's lips against mine made me feel dizzy and I was glad his hand was behind me. *That* was the kiss I'd been expecting since I'd been back on campus. We hadn't lost any of our sparkle over the summer—it had all been in my head.

24
AND THE GOLD MEDAL
GOES TO . . .

I TROTTED CHARM AROUND THE INDOOR arena, feeling better than I had since the first day of school. Rain pounded the roof, making it sound as if more than three horses were warming up.

I hadn't stopped feeling sparkly since my kiss with Eric. Tomorrow night was going to be *amazing* and I had to stop worrying about problems that didn't even exist. Before the lesson, I'd put on my new breeches—plum-colored ones with suede knees—and was wearing my fave white shirt with a tiny pocket. I felt like me—like I knew what I was doing and could handle today's lesson.

Jas trotted Phoenix up to me. I ignored her and stared ahead.

"Awww, trying to focus for once?" Jas asked.

I turned to look at her. "Awww, trying to throw me off much?" I asked, my tone mocking hers.

Jas's eyes narrowed. Phoenix and Charm trotted faster, matching each other stride for stride. Before Jas could deliver a comeback, Mr. Conner entered the arena.

Jasmine checked Phoenix and dropped him back behind Charm. Ahead of me, Heather slowed Aristocrat. Mr. Conner walked into the arena and stopped in the center.

"Hi, girls," he said. "Please drop your stirrups and cross them."

Heather and I looked at each other—this was going to be intense. Jasmine, Heather, and I secured our stirrups and waited for instructions.

"Start at a sitting trot and make large figure eights, crossing through the arena's center," Mr. Conner said.

I eased Charm into a trot and sat deep in the saddle, gripping with my knees to prevent bouncing. We followed behind Aristocrat and the darker chestnut bent through the moves with ease. Charm followed behind him. I was glad I couldn't see Jasmine for most of the exercise.

"Nice, Sasha," Mr. Conner called out. I smiled, but stayed focused. Finally! This was how Charm and I were supposed to perform during lessons.

We made three more figure eights. With each repetition,

I felt myself loosen up and my hips and back flexed. He was so getting a giant carrot after this.

"Larger figure eights at a slow canter," Mr. Conner said.

I gave Charm extra rein and within two strides, he started to canter. Overhead, the rain slammed into the roof and almost drowned out the sounds of hoofbeats. The movement of Charm's canter and the soft overhead lights made me relax.

"Slow to a walk," Mr. Conner called.

We walked for a couple of laps and Charm was quiet—listening and waiting for a cue from me.

"Sitting trot for half a lap, then canter," Mr. Conner said.

I squeezed my legs against Charm's sides and pushed my seat into the saddle. Charm trotted and snorted, pulling his head down. He'd seen Aristocrat and Phoenix already start to canter and he wanted to go. I corrected him and made him trot for an extra lap before asking him to canter.

"Good call, Sasha," Mr. Conner said.

We made two circuits around the arena before Mr. Conner asked us to stop. "I want to move to the other end of the arena and work the horses through some gymnastics."

Heather, Jasmine, and I guided the horses behind Mr. Conner.

Ten rails had been lined up—all about six inches off the ground.

"These are spaced close together on purpose," Mr. Conner explained. "But they're low and you'll trot through the course." He moved away from us and over to the side of the course to watch.

"Omigod," Jas hissed. "Trotting over those tiny jumps?"

Heather and I ignored her. I couldn't think of one lesson when Jas hadn't complained. She wasn't a giant fan of practicing—she lived to compete.

"Sasha," Mr. Conner said. "You can go first."

I trotted Charm over to the start of the course and guided him in front of the first rail. He jumped it easily, trotted a few more strides and took the second rail. He bounced through the gymnastics and kept an even stride throughout. At the end of the course, I patted Charm's neck and slowed him to a walk.

Mr. Conner nodded at us and motioned to Heather to go ahead. Heather and Aristocrat moved smoothly through the course. Aristocrat seemed to like the gymnastics— he tossed his head at the end of the course as if he wanted to go again.

Jas's lips were pressed together and she glowered as she watched Heather rejoin us.

For the rest of the lesson, I kept my attention on Charm and we were a team again. When Mr. Conner raised his hand to signal the end of the lesson, I was sorry to stop. I'd even forgotten that there hadn't been stirrups! It felt good to be back in the zone.

"Great job, girls," Mr. Conner said. He looked at each of us. "I've noticed improvements in all of your hands and legs over the past couple of lessons. Please care for your horses and I'll see you at the next lesson."

I uncrossed my stirrups, dismounted, and then ran them up.

"You were *great*, boy," I told Charm. "I'm so proud of you." I loosened his girth and pulled the reins over his head.

I hugged him and started walking him in lazy circles around the arena. Maybe I'd been reading into things too much all this time. Tomorrow was my birthday, Eric and I were happy and my best friends were there for me. I'd been dreading the party because I felt so guilty about what I was doing, but it was time to let myself off the hook. Every lie I'd told was for a good reason.

25

JUST ONE WISH

THE CALM I'D FELT LAST NIGHT ABOUT THE party? Gone.

It was starting in less than an hour and I was *freaking*. I'd already dropped my hair dryer (a little too close to a sink full of water, eep!), tripped over my desk chair leg, and flatironed my hair so many times, I was lucky to have any hair left that wasn't singed.

"Sasha," Paige asked. "Are you *sure* you're okay? Did you have an espresso again?"

"I'm fine," I said. "No coffee. Just nervous—it's my birthday party and I want everyone to have fun."

"They will," Paige said. She pulled on a casual black pocket dress and smoothed out the front. "Remember who planned the party."

I smiled. "This is true. Any party of Paige Parker's is always fun."

I picked up my own dress off my bed and put it on. It was a tank dress with a white top and tiered black bottom. I slipped my feet into my heels—I'd managed to convince Mom to let me buy kitten heels over the summer. They were shiny black peep-toe heels with tiny bows. I still had to do my makeup, but I wanted to get used to wearing the heels. I did *not* want to make an entrance by tripping as I walked through the door.

"Ready for makeup?" Paige asked.

I was in her desk chair in seconds. "Yes!"

Paige took out her makeup bag, which wouldn't even close anymore, and got to work.

"I'm trying a plum eyeshadow, since purple is supposed to enhance green eyes," she said. "Okay?"

"Of course," I said. "I totally trust Jade."

Paige grinned. "And Kiki can do me next."

Paige and I had been using makeup-artist names since the first time we'd done each other's makeup.

I sat back in the chair, trying to breathe and not let Paige see how nervous I was. She applied a light coat of moisturizer, evened out my skin with a sheer foundation, and applied a coat of peachy-rose–colored blush. She used black liquid eyeliner on my top eyelids and then brushed on the eye shadow.

"Clear gloss and you're party-ready," Paige said, stepping back and studying my face. "You look totally gorgeous."

I peered into the mirror. "Paige, you should be charging for this. Seriously. Now you sit."

Paige sat down and I picked the different shades and colors I wanted for her. Her ivory skin didn't need foundation, so I dotted concealer under her eyes. I grabbed a soft-gray shadow that would complement her red hair. I dipped the skinny brush into the eye shadow.

"You're shaking," Paige said. "What's wrong?"

"I'm just so excited!" I said. "It's my *thirteenth* birthday party. Now close your eyes."

Paige glanced at me for a second, but finally nodded. "Okay. But seriously, don't worry about anything. I've got everything under control—all you have to do is show up."

"I know," I said. "You've gone above and beyond to throw me what I *know* is going to be an awesome party. I really, really appreciate it, Paige."

She smiled at me. "You're my best friend. Of course I'd do this for you—you know that. And Callie helped a lot too."

"I know," I said. "Now close your eyes."

When Paige's eyes were shut, I took another breath and willed myself to stop shaking. Everything was going to be fine. I worked hard to keep my hand steady as I brushed eye shadow along Paige's eyelids.

"Okay," I said a few minutes later. "Check it out."

Paige got up and looked in the mirror. "Uh, I think I should pay *you*. Maybe we should just go into business together."

We giggled and did last-minute hair checks. I applied a final coat of gloss—Lip Glam in Berry Glisten. "Use this," I said, passing it to Paige. "It'll look even better on you with your skin color."

Paige brushed the wand over her lips and rubbed them together. "This does look good. Thanks." She handed it back to me.

"Ready?" I asked. I just wanted to get the party started and end it as early as possible.

"Ready."

Paige and I walked down the hallway to the Winchester common room. Paige hurried to get in front of me and placed her hand on the doorknob.

"Happy birthday, Sasha. I really hope you like everything," she said.

"Paige." I hugged her. "I'm going to love it. Open the door already!"

With a final grin at me, Paige pulled open the door and waved me inside. I stepped into a room that looked *nothing* like the Winchester common room. Paige had transformed it from cozy chic to modern and cool with a black-and-white theme. Bottles of sparkling cider were chilling in an ice bucket on the counter and a dozen champagne flutes were ready to be filled.

"Paaaige," I said. "This is amazing!" There were black and white candles everywhere. Paige had brought in clear vases and had filled them with origami black and white flowers. Only when I stopped gaping at the decorations did I notice the people inside.

"Happy birthday," Troy said, walking over to hug me.

"Thanks!" I said. "Glad you came."

I looked over and saw Jasmine in the corner talking to Alison. Neither girl looked as if she was about to kill the other. I wondered if everyone would be able to play it cool tonight. Julia was surveying the snack table with Nicole, Annabella, and Suichin.

Andy, Ben, and Ryan walked in together and each guy put a present on the gift table Paige had set up. There was already a massive pile of presents—boxes, bags, and cards—almost spilling off the table. It was a colorful explosion of ribbons and wrapping paper.

"Sasha!" Callie and Jacob walked in holding hands and Callie released his hand to hug me. "Happy birthday!"

"Thanks!" I hugged her back, avoiding Jacob's gaze. "Paige told me you helped a lot, so really, thank you."

"Please," Callie said. "I got party-planning lessons from a pro. It was awesome."

"Happy birthday," Jacob said.

"Thanks." I half smiled at him, then we both looked away from each other.

Callie looked gorgeous and perfect for a summer party. She wore a creamy colored skirt that hit just above her knees and a black tank top with lacy straps.

"Paige did an amazing job with the decorations," Callie said. "The black-and-white theme is so cool. She told me what to do and I just followed her directions." She turned to Jacob. "Do you like it?"

Jacob nodded. "Yeah, you guys did a great job." He looked away and tipped his head at Troy and the other guys who were on the couch stuffing their faces. "I'm gonna go talk to them for a sec," he said to Callie.

"Okay," she said.

Jacob walked away and Callie turned to me. "Omigod,

this is going to the best party ever. You've got a zillion presents and everyone's here just for you."

"Except Eric," I said. "But he should be here any second. Let's get some sparkling cider while we wait for him."

We grabbed two champagne flutes and I lifted the cider out of the silver ice bucket.

"Allow me."

I turned to find Eric standing behind Callie and me.

"Hey!" I said, wrapping my arms around him.

"Happy birthday, Sasha," he said in my ear.

He took the cider from me and poured glasses for Callie and me before filling a glass for himself.

"Let's toast," Callie said. "To my best friend on her thirteenth birthday. I hope you have the wonderful night that you deserve!"

"Cheers!" Eric said. We raised our glasses and clinked them together. I looked at them and finally felt completely secure—this was going to be the best party ever.

Jacob headed toward us and my heart started beating faster.

"Um, let's go try Paige's food," I said to Callie. I grabbed her arm and pulled her toward the snack table, almost causing her to spill her drink.

Callie and I walked over to the table with a black table-cloth that sparkled with silver glitter. Paige had made a variety of sandwiches cut into tiny triangles, a cheese plate, and fruit salad.

While Callie and I put food on our plates, I kept one eye on everyone else. Jas had moved to get a glass of cider, Eric and Jacob were at opposite ends of the room, Paige was floating from group to group playing hostess, and Callie was with me. Phew!

Callie and I sat on the couch and indulged in Paige's food.

"She could drop out of school today and go full time on The Food Network for Kids," Callie said.

"I know," I said. "She could. These cucumber sand-wiches are amazing."

Callie finished her food and started to stand. I shoved the rest of my fruit salad in my mouth, starting to jump up after her.

"Saaasha!" Nicole, my friend from the stable, said as she stepped up to me. "Happy birthday!"

"Thanks," I said. I started to weave around her to fol-low Callie in case she went to talk to Eric, but Nicole reached out to hug me.

"I'm so glad school started early this year so we could

do this," she said. She pushed a blond curl from her face. "Isn't it great to be back?"

But I barely heard her. I watched Callie go over to Andy and Ben, laughing at something they said. "It's great," I echoed. "So good to be back."

"I haven't seen you once at the stable," Nicole said, playing with the star pendant that dangled around her neck. "Wish probably misses Charm. We should trail ride together soon."

"Mmm hmm."

Jasmine left the cider table and headed for Eric. Jas had *nothing* on me, but I didn't want her alone with Eric.

"Gotta go!" I said, darting around Nicole. "Talk to you later."

I hurried across the floor, appearing at Eric's side just as Jasmine stopped in front of him. And, omigod, was I sweating?

"Where did you *come* from?" Jasmine asked, staring at me. "Did you seriously just run over here to get between me and your boyfriend?"

Jas looked stunning in a black minidress with silver kitten heels. Her dark wavy hair was loose and her makeup job rivaled Paige's.

I slid my arm around Eric's waist. "Yeah, that's *exactly*

what I did. But can we not? It's my party and if you're not here to have fun, then you should feel free to leave."

Jas rolled her eyes. "Like I'm really going to stay? Puh-lease. I just came to see if anyone would actually show up. After cake, I'm out of here."

Jas took a step back and turned around just as Heather walked into the room. She carried a purple gift bag in one hand and a black purse in the other.

"So, Heather really can make people nervous with-out doing or saying anything," Eric whispered in my ear. "Amazing."

"I know." We laughed and I let go of him. "I've got to go say hi. But come find me in five minutes if I don't come back, 'kay?"

Eric nodded. "Make it two."

Smiling to myself, I started over toward Heather. I was edgy after running around to watch everyone, but I was hav-ing fun and it seemed like everyone else was too. Someone turned up the music on the iPod speakers and Julia and Ben started dancing in the open space behind the couch.

"Thanks for coming," I said to Heather. Her blond hair was straightened and pulled back in a half updo. She looked superglam in a strapless tube dress that almost matched my eye shadow.

She handed me the gift bag. "Happy birthday." Her blue eyes studied my face. "Oh, Silver." She let out an exaggerated sigh. "What's going on? Did our BFF Jas do something that gives me an excuse to pour a drink on her and kick her out?"

I stared at her and my fake everything's-great-and-awesome attitude fell for a second. How was it that after hanging out with so many people tonight, Heather was the first one to see something was wrong?

"I wish," I said. "I'd love to give you a reason to toss Jas. But nothing's wrong. Everything's fine."

"Fine?" Heather stepped closer and lowered her voice. "Everything 'fine' at your thirteenth birthday party?"

"Yes," I squeaked. I couldn't look her in the eyes. I was afraid that if I did, I'd spill all of my worries about tonight onto her. They would pour out and wouldn't stop. The urge to confess to Heather was disturbing. She was the leader of the Trio! "I didn't mean to say 'fine.' I meant that the party is fantastic. Go get a drink or something."

Heather looked at me for another second. She obviously didn't believe me.

"Okay," she said. She leaned in toward my ear. "But *only* because it's your birthday—if you need . . . help with something, find me."

She walked away, leaving me clutching the gift bag and shaking my head. I put the present on the table with the rest of the gifts and walked past Paige. She'd migrated to the kitchen area of the common room and was talking to Ryan. She grinned at me as I walked by and I winked at her. She was getting more comfortable with him every time they got together.

"I think you were gone longer than two minutes," Eric said, grabbing me from behind and wrapping his arms around me. I laughed and turned around, looking into his face. He quickly kissed me and took my hand. "C'mere."

I followed him through the room and he pushed open the door, leading me out into the quiet hallway.

"Eric!" I said. "I can't leave my own party. Everyone's in there."

Everyone was here for me and all I could do was try not to have a meltdown because of my lies. What if Jacob just decided to confess everything and tell them the truth? But I knew that was dumb the second I thought it—they were all exactly where they'd been when I'd left the room two seconds ago.

"You're not leaving," Eric said. "You're ducking. For two minutes." He reached into his back pocket and produced a tiny white box tied with a simple black ribbon. "I wanted to be the first one to give you a present on your birthday."

"Eric." I took the box from him and slid off the silky ribbon. I opened the lid of the box and inside was a silver charm for my bracelet. A *heart*. I touched the charm and looked up at him. "It's *perfect*. This is the best gift any-one's ever given me."

I held out my wrist to Eric and let him fasten the charm next to the horseshoe one he'd given me on our first date.

"Good," he said. "Because you're special to me."

I leaned over to put the box on the hallway table, check-ing behind me for Livvie. But the hall was empty.

I stepped up to Eric until our faces were inches apart. I rested my arms on the tops of his shoulders.

"You having a good birthday so far?" Eric asked.

"The best," I said.

He leaned closer and my eyes fluttered shut. Our lips had barely touched when I heard a door open behind us.

Jacob stood in the hallway, his hands shoved into his pockets. I took a step away from Eric and my face went pink.

"Sorry," Jacob said after what felt like hours. He stared

at the hallway floor. "Paige was looking for you—she wants to cut the cake."

"Go ahead," I said to Eric. "I'll be right there. I need to run to the bathroom for a quick hair check before we have cake. Paige will be putting all of our pics on FaceSpace."

"Okay," Eric said, squeezing my hand. "See you inside."

Eric didn't even look at Jacob as he brushed past him. The door closed, leaving me with Jacob.

Jacob and I stared at each other. He opened his mouth to say something, then his eyes landed on my wrist. Still peering at my bracelet, he stepped forward and took my hand.

"Jacob—" I started, but the look on his face stopped me.

Jacob raised my hand so the bracelet dangled in the air and his eyes locked on the heart charm. I wasn't sure if it was pain, sadness, surprise, or all of those things that flashed on his face and made my heart twist.

"Did he just give that to you?" Jacob's voice was barely audible.

"Yes." My own voice was a whisper.

Jacob didn't let go of my hand. "Did you want it?"

I started to say that of course I did. Eric was my

boyfriend and I liked him so much. But nothing came out. I yanked my hand away from Jacob and hurried around him to go inside. I let the door slam behind me.

"There's the birthday girl," Paige said, rushing up to me. She took the hand that Jacob had just held and guided me toward the counter.

Nicole, Annabella, and Suichin stepped aside, waving their arms with flourish. On the counter was a three-tiered square cake. Each layer was shaped like a present with white wrapping paper and pink ribbons and bows.

"Paige," I said, gasping. "Did you *make* that?"

"Yeah," Paige said. "I wasn't going to trust anyone else with my best friend's birthday cake. Everything's edible—bows and ribbons—all of it."

I hugged her but couldn't take my eyes off the cake. "It's just beyond gorgeous. Omigod."

Ryan pulled out his camera. "Let's take a pic of us with the cake before we eat it so Paige has a photo."

"I'd love that," Paige said, smiling at Ryan.

Ryan put his camera on a high shelf and set it on a timer, and a red light started flashing. "Ten seconds for everyone to get in the shot," he said.

We scrambled to pose around the cake. Paige and Callie threw their arms around me, Eric got behind me, and everyone else huddled together. We grinned and the flash went off.

Ryan grabbed his camera and checked the screen. "Perfect."

Paige arranged thirteen pink candles on the cake and grabbed a lighter.

"I got Livvie's permission," she said quickly when she saw my eyes widen. "But you're not allowed to touch the lighter. I promised her."

I raised my hands in an I'm-backing-off gesture and grinned.

Ryan took a pic of her lighting all of the candles.

All of my friends huddled around me. Someone turned down the lights and everyone looked at me. I felt like I was swaying in the room. They were all here for me and I'd been lying to my best friend, keeping secrets from my other BFF, and hiding things from my boyfriend. I knew exactly why I was doing these things, but at that moment I felt like a loser.

"Happy birthday to you," everyone began to sing.

Their faces started to blur in front of me. The candle lights flickered and danced on the walls. I found myself looking for someone's face. But he wasn't there.

Jacob.

Calm down, I told myself. What did I want from him? Jacob liked me and he'd just seen a heart charm from my boyfriend. He was probably hurt. My stomach ached. I didn't want Jacob to be upset, but there was nothing I could do. The party was almost over. I'd figure out another way to deal with the lies after tonight and a way to talk to Jacob. I'd tell Paige everything, she wouldn't transfer my boy drama onto Ryan, and I'd be able to stop worrying every five seconds.

"...toooo yoooooouu!" everyone finished the song and started clapping.

I squeezed my eyes shut and thought, *I wish I knew how to fix everything.* I blew out the candles.

"Yay!" Paige said. "Let's eat cake!"

Eric helped Paige remove the candles and he grabbed a knife.

I leaned over to Paige's ear. "I'm going to the bathroom. I'll be right back."

"'Kay," she said. "I'm giving you the biggest piece of cake. Then you can unwrap presents."

"Awesome." I smiled and walked out of the common room, away from the music and laughter.

26

I CAN'T STAY AWAY
FROM YOU

I WALKED DOWN THE HALLWAY AND OPENED
the door to my room. I left the door ajar and sat at the
edge of my bed. The stress of worrying if someone was
going to find out my real feelings—not to mention
my lies—was more than I could handle. *That's why you
decided to tell Paige tomorrow instead of waiting till fall break,*
I reminded myself. Confiding in her would make me
feel less alone and maybe Paige would have an idea to
help me fix everything.

But I knew it wasn't just up to Paige. I was going to
have to think about my feelings for Eric and Jacob. I
couldn't deal with it now and I hadn't been able to all
summer, but I'd have to sooner or later.

I reached over to swipe the papaya Stila lip gloss that

Callie had given me on my first date with Eric. I applied some gloss and when I looked up, Jacob was standing in the doorway.

"Jacob, if Livvie catches you in my room, she's gonna freak. You need to go."

Jacob shook his head. "I'll go. But I want to talk to you first."

He walked over and sat beside me on my bed. He stared at his hands for a long time before looking up at me. "I miss you, Sasha. I'll tell you again that I made a huge mistake and I'm sorry. I wish you would have e-mailed me or something over the summer, but I get it why you didn't. I ignored you for a long time after the Sweetheart Soirée."

"Jacob—"

He stopped me with a raised hand. "I know you're with another guy. I'm trying to respect that. But . . . I can't stay away from you."

"Do you realize what position you've put me in?" I asked. "I've had to keep this from Callie—it would kill her. I obviously couldn't tell Eric. When you told me that you still liked me, it put a lot of pressure on me to keep that secret from everyone."

Jacob lowered his head. "I know. I didn't think about it

before I said it. But I had to tell you. I couldn't have spent all summer regretting that I didn't."

I rubbed my forehead with my hand. "I'm with Eric. He's my boyfriend now. I like him, Jacob. A lot. And you're with Callie. She's so into you and I know you like her."

Jacob's green eyes settled on my face. "Admit that you still like me. Just tell me the truth. Please."

Panic and guilt fluttered in my chest. We couldn't be sitting in my room having this conversation.

"Jacob, no," I said. "I can't—"

Jacob leaned forward and pressed his lips to mine. I froze for a second, shocked, then put my hands on his chest and pushed him back.

Something moved in the doorway and I looked over.

Eric.

My hands were still on Jacob's chest. I yanked them off and stood. "Eric," I started. "I—"

The look on his face stopped me.

He didn't look surprised. It was way worse than surprise—as if he'd expected it. Like he'd known it was coming all along.

"Why did I *ever* think it would happen any other way?" Eric's voice was calm. "You were about to kiss him. Why stop now?"

He hadn't seen the kiss! There was still a chance that I could explain this away somehow.

"Eric," I said again. But he held up his hand and I saw the anger in his eyes.

He stared at me and his gaze almost made me sink back onto the bed.

"I knew this would happen," Eric said. "I knew it, but I tried to convince myself that it was just me. That you really liked me. I can't believe you, Sasha. I *always* knew you'd go back to him."

Eric's eyes shifted to Jacob. There was a quiet anger on his face. I knew not to say another word. Eric turned and walked away.

I couldn't even breathe. I stood there, staring at the doorway wanting more than anything to run after him, but knowing it would only make things worse.

I turned to Jacob. "You ruined *everything*! My relationship with Eric is over." I tried to keep from screaming at him.

"You were over a long time ago," Jacob said. "You just won't admit it."

"So what do you want me to do?" My voice rose. "Admit that I'm confused about my feelings for you? Then what? You leave my best friend for me?"

Jacob got off the bed and stood in front of me. "Yes. We can have the chance we never got. I'll find a way to break it off with Callie and we can start over."

I put my head in my hands, then looked back up at him. "No. You can't break up with her for me. She likes you so much. Our friendship would *never* recover if you did that."

"I'd find a way that wouldn't hurt her. And I'm not hearing you say you want to go back to Eric."

I paused. He was right—I hadn't said that.

"Because it's not even a question," I said. "I've hurt him enough. He'll never take me back after this. If you care about me like you say you do, then you'll stay with Callie and never tell her about this. Ever."

Jacob shook his head. "I can't do that. Sasha, how can I let you go again?"

I had to chew on the inside of my mouth to keep from crying. "I'm going back to my party," I said. "Paige worked hard on it. No one's going to know what just happened. Eric won't tell anyone—he'd never risk my friendship with Callie, no matter how mad he is."

Jacob dropped his head, then looked back at me. "You really want me to go back to Callie and pretend not to like you?"

"Yes. Or break up with her, if that's what you really want, but not for me. I can't be with you—not ever. Not after you've been Callie's boyfriend. She'd never forgive me. And Eric was the perfect boyfriend. He didn't deserve this."

Jacob and I fell silent.

"Okay," he said finally. "If that's what you really want, if it means that much to you, I'll do it. Just know that it's you I'll always be wishing for. I'll never tell Callie—don't ever worry about that. And *never* say a guy doesn't deserve you, Sasha."

I blinked back tears and walked around Jacob, leaving him behind.

27

NO GOING BACK

I PAUSED OUTSIDE THE COMMON ROOM, holding back tears and taking deep breaths. All I had to do was get through presents and then I could escape. I wasn't going to ruin this party for everyone. I'd done enough of that before. I pasted a fake smile on my face and walked inside.

Paige and Callie were standing together by the gift table.

"Ready to open presents?" Callie asked, smiling at me.

"Definitely," I said. I tried to keep from looking directly at Paige or Callie so they wouldn't see how upset I was.

Paige looked around. "Everyone's still here except for Jacob—he disappeared. But I'm sure he won't mind if you start opening them."

Callie nodded. "He'll understand. Open!"

Everyone in the room turned to watch me, curious about what I'd gotten. Andy turned down the music and everyone's attention was on me.

I reached for the present closest to me—Heather's gift bag. I started to pull out the purple tissue paper that fanned out of the opening when Jasmine stepped up to the other side of the table.

"Wow," she said, shaking her head.

I looked over at her. "What?"

Jas smiled widely and her eyes didn't leave mine. "I'm just *shocked* that you feel up to opening presents after that."

"After what?" Paige asked, frowning at Jas.

"After what? Oh, I'm sorry." Jasmine covered her mouth with one hand. "Sasha, did you not tell your BFFs what just happened? Omigod, I thought you did. I'm *so* sorry."

I gripped the table for support.

Jasmine knew.

"What's she talking about?" Callie asked. "What's wrong?"

I stood—staring at Callie and Paige—not able to say a word.

Jacob, silent, walked into the room and sat on the couch.

Callie reached over and touched my arm. "You look sick. What happened?" She looked over and seemed to remember that the room was full of people. "Want to go in the hallway and talk or something?"

Jasmine smirked. "I don't think *you* want to be alone with Sasha when she tells you what happened."

I shut my eyes for a second and tried to stop things from feeling swirly. I had to do something to stop Jas—to end this. I'd lost Eric. I could never be with Jacob. Paige was going to be furious with me for lying. Callie was about to hate me.

But I could keep Callie with Jacob. One final lie and Callie and I would never be friends again, but she'd have him.

I forced myself to look at Callie and let go of the table. I had to make every word convincing so that she wouldn't doubt any of it. Not one bit of blame could fall on Jacob.

"I went to my room," I said, my voice flat. "Jacob walked by and I asked him to come inside. He thought I was upset about something and needed to talk."

Out of the corner of my eye, I saw Jacob shift on the couch. I silently willed him not to move and to let me do this.

"Okay, so you talked to Jacob," Callie shrugged. "I don't care."

"He sat down on my bed," I continued. I kept my eyes locked on Callie. "And I told him I'd wanted him back for months. That I still liked him and wanted him to break up with you and be with me."

The room went silent. Callie's and Paige's mouths fell open. I forced myself to keep a cold look on my face— doing what I'd seen Heather and Jasmine do so many times. Heather moved beside Jasmine and looked at me. She knew I was lying. Somehow, she just knew. For a split second, I looked at Jacob and saw his face pale. I had to keep going before he stopped me.

"You *what*?" Callie sputtered.

I fought to keep from sobbing. Lie by lie, I was destroying my relationship with my best friend. There was no going back after this. Callie would never trust me again. But I couldn't stop.

"Jacob realized I didn't really have anything to talk about and he got up, but I grabbed his arm and pulled him back."

Callie's eyes squeezed shut and tears slid down her face. She looked as if she wasn't even breathing.

I wanted Callie to believe it. Every detail would make

her hate me more. I had to keep going before I broke down.

"I put my hands on his chest and went to kiss him," I said. "He started to push me away and Eric walked in. He saw me with Jacob, left, and Jacob told me to get out so he could figure out what to do."

Callie looked at Jacob. "Do you want her back?"

Jacob's face was paler than I'd ever seen it. He was careful not to glance at me, but I could see the pain in his eyes. He knew I was destroying my friendship with Callie.

Jacob got up and walked over to Callie, looking into her eyes. He was almost unsteady on his feet for the first couple of steps. "No."

Paige shook her head slowly. "This doesn't make any sense. I know you, Sasha. You'd *never* do this to anyone. You're covering. Something else is going on."

"No," I said. "I'm not." I had to make Paige believe me.

Paige just stared at me for what felt like hours. She walked toward me, stopping long enough to lean by my ear. "I don't believe a word of this. I don't know what you're doing, but I'm going to figure it out." She walked out of the room and Annabella hurried after her.

Across the table, Jasmine clapped. The sound was deafening in the room.

"Now *this* is a party!" she said. "I'm so glad I didn't miss it."

Heather stuck her face in Jas's. "Get. Out. Now."

Jasmine widened her eyes and put a hand on her hip. "Excuse me. I'm not—"

"*Now,*" Heather said. "Everyone but Callie and Sasha get out of here before I make you leave."

No one needed to be told twice by Heather. But Jacob was the last one to leave. I could feel him wanting to stay—wanting to tell the truth. But he finally left and the room emptied.

Callie and I, still on opposite sides of the table, stared at each other. I wasn't sure if she was going to sob or scream at me.

I kept my face expressionless. I'd gone this far—I had to hurt her enough that she believed every word.

"You . . . ," Callie started. Her voice shook and tears spilled down her cheeks. I struggled to keep my composure, but I was about to start crying at any second. "You know this is it. We're done. We will *never* be friends again. I don't care if you apologize for the rest of your life. I'll never forgive you for this."

A sob rose in my throat, but I held it down.

Callie started crying. She slammed her palms on the tabletop, then swiped at her tears, smearing mascara across her face. I wanted to run around the table, hug her, and tell her the truth. That it had been Jacob. Not me. That I wanted to be her best friend. That I'd been confused, but would never have gone after her boyfriend.

But instead, I stood there watching my best friend cry. I didn't move.

"We just got our friendship back, Sasha," Callie said. "That meant everything to me. You were my best friend. I would have done anything for you. And you went after Jacob? I'll never speak to you again."

I had to say something—anything that would wipe any possible trace of doubt from her mind when she went through this over and over in her head tonight.

"It was worth it," I heard myself say. It felt like it was coming out of someone else's mouth. "Losing our friendship was worth it for a shot at Jacob."

My own words made me sick. My stomach swirled and my face started to turn red. This had to end now before I blew it and told her the truth.

Callie swallowed, wiping tears from her face. "I'm

glad," she said. "I hope you're happy alone. I *hate* you and I never want to see you again."

Callie walked around the table and I kept my back to her as she left the room. The door slammed shut behind her. I crumpled to the floor, sobbing.

I'd just given up my best friend to protect her. And in the process, I'd lost everyone. I was alone—just like I'd been on my first day at Canterwood.

ABOUT THE AUTHOR

Twenty-two-year-old Jessica Burkhart is a writer from New York City. Like Sasha, she's crazy about horses, lip gloss, and all things pink and sparkly. Jess was an equestrian and had a horse like Charm before she started writing. To watch Jess's vlogs and read her blog, visit www.jessicaburkhart.com.

MEET BRITTANY, CASSIE, AND ISABEL. THREE GIRLS WITH BIG DREAMS AND BIG AMBITIONS.

Sometimes the drama during the commercials is better than what happens during the show. And sometimes the drama making the commercial is even better. . . .

Do you love the color pink?
All things sparkly? Mani/pedis?

These books are for you!

From Aladdin
Published by Simon & Schuster

Sometimes a girl just needs a good book.
Lauren Barnholdt understands.

www.laurenbarnholdt.com

From Aladdin M!X   Published by Simon & Schuster

Get lost in these international adventures

Learn more at aladdinmix.com!

From Aladdin   KIDS.SimonandSchuster.com